Summerspell

SUMMERSPELL

Jean Thesman

Simon & Schuster Books for Young Readers

 SIMON & SCHUSTER BOOKS FOR YOUNG READERS
An imprint of Simon & Schuster Children's Publishing Division
1230 Avenue of the Americas
New York, NY 10020
Text copyright © 1995 by Jean Thesman
SIMON & SCHUSTER BOOKS FOR YOUNG READERS is a trademark of Simon & Schuster.
Designed by Virginia Pope.
The text of this book is set in Berkeley.
Manufactured in the United States of America
10 9 8 7 6 5 4 3 2 1

Library of Congress Cataloging-in-Publication Data
Thesman, Jean.
Summerspell / Jean Thesman.
p. cm.
Summary: While living with her sister, fifteen-year-old Jocelyn has trouble with her hateful brother-in-law and runs away to her family's summer cabin, where the unwanted presence of two boys complicates her plan of escape.
ISBN: 0-671-50130-5
[1. Runaways—Fiction. 2. Lakes—Fiction. 3. Sexual harassment—Fiction.]
I. Title. II. Title: Summerspell.
PZ7.T3525Su 1995 [Fic]—dc20   94-25737

This is for Cassie, who knows all the reasons why

$\mathcal{O}$NE

$\mathcal{Y}$ou probably heard about me. I'm Jocelyn Tyler. I ran away from my sister's house one Friday when I was fifteen, and what happened before that day was, in part, my fault. I admit I did my best to get even with Gerald. But the things that happened afterward—the things that put my name and picture in the newspapers—couldn't have been my fault. At least, that's what I try telling myself in the daylight hours.

Yet sometimes, in the darkest part of the night when I can't sleep, I remember Baily, Spider, and me in the boat that last time, and I cringe. Now I can see all the places I might have been wrong, the times I should have stayed silent. And the times I should have spoken out.

There are some secrets that need to be kept. But there are others that should be shouted at every street corner until someone listens. I wish I had always known the difference.

The bus wasn't scheduled to leave until ten minutes after eight that Friday, but I boarded as soon as I bought a ticket.

I avoided making eye contact with other passengers, and moved quickly to an aisle seat in the back, next to an elderly woman who had already made herself comfortable with a book.

The woman glanced up over her glasses, surprised when I sat down. There were so many empty places—naturally she would wonder why a stranger had taken the one next to her. But I didn't dare sit by a window, where I might easily be seen by someone searching for me.

I stuffed my duffel bag under my seat and opened the paperback book I had bought at the newsstand inside the bus station. In my panic, I had already forgotten the title, and the print danced before my eyes. Someone passing in the aisle bumped my head, but I didn't look up. I hadn't been hurt—but the person hadn't apologized, either.

The bus was ancient and smelled of dust and dirty socks and the old woman's lavender cologne. A small headache began above my eyes.

I checked my watch, then looked back at my book, but I couldn't concentrate on the story. My heart beat uncomfortably hard. Was running away the right thing to do? Maybe it wasn't too late to change my mind. No, no, I couldn't go back.

By five minutes to eight, the bus was half full. A man sitting near the front began coughing when the bus in the next bay pulled out, gushing diesel fumes.

I checked my watch again. Eight o'clock exactly.

"It'll leave on time," the woman next to me said. "I take this trip once a month, and the bus always leaves on time."

I didn't respond. I was afraid she might ask questions, and even though I had planned all the lies I thought I could possibly need, silence was safer.

One last passenger got on. *Baily!*

His bright blue gaze found me instantly, and he took a seat two rows away. I narrowed my eyes but didn't speak. If he says one word, I told myself, I'll get off the bus, no matter how it upsets my plans.

He must have seen how angry I was, because he looked away from me and out the window, and his clear tanned face flushed.

I could see I'd made a mistake calling him from the convenience store the night before to tell him that Gerald had cut down the tree with the heron's nest. He and his father had done their best to protect the bird from Gerald's plans to build his new church there, but Gerald was crazy, really crazy. I'd told Baily I couldn't take any more and was running away. Stupidly, I'd even told him the plans I'd made moments before, when I called Gran-auntie in San Francisco. So here he was on the bus, putting himself in danger in case Gerald caught me, and causing me even more panic.

At last the driver closed the door and eased the bus into the heavy downtown Seattle traffic. I bent lower over my book. By now my half-sister, Hope, and her husband, Gerald, would know I was gone. Would they come in from the suburbs to look for me in the bus depot? Probably not, at least not this soon. But my luck had been worse than usual lately. Proof enough of that was Baily's presence on the bus.

He'd been a better friend than I deserved, ever since I moved to Seattle to stay with my sister. But at that moment he presented a bigger problem than I was ready to handle.

The August morning sun shone full on the woman next to the window as the bus rolled north on the freeway. She shielded her face with one hand, sighed, and said, "I hate sitting in the sun. Excuse me, dear. I have to change seats."

I swung my legs to the side to let the woman pass. "Excuse me," I heard her say to someone else a moment later. "Excuse me. Do you mind if I sit here?"

Baily moved to the seat the woman had left.

"Jocelyn..." he began.

"Let me alone," I whispered. "You shouldn't have done this. You have to go back."

"I can't," he said. "Gary Prescott's family is leaving for the ocean today, and I told my parents I'd decided to go with them after all."

"Stupid," I hissed. "You think they believed you? I bet you even told your dad that Gerald destroyed the heron's nest."

"No, I didn't. And my parents don't suspect anything. Dad left for the office early, and Mom gave me fifty bucks for spending money. Satisfied?"

"You're not coming with me," I said. "That's final."

"I'm here, and *that's* final."

Baily liked me too much. I'd known that for a long time, and I felt guilty about it. And here he was, tagging along like a puppy. If my luck failed, and Gerald found me with Baily, he'd go out of control. My brother-in-law, who was the preacher at Holy Brethren Tabernacle, didn't even let me date. And he hated Baily because he was so good-looking.

"I know what dirty things he's got on his mind," Gerald had said. "I'll see him in hell before I ever let him touch you."

Baily didn't deserve what might happen if Gerald ever found out he'd run away with me.

"Please get off the first time the bus stops," I whispered. "Please, Baily."

He shook his head, and refused to look at me.

It took half an hour to reach the city limits. I shoved my denim jacket under my seat, leaned my head back, and shut my eyes. Was I safe? Not yet. But every mile I put between myself and home made me safer from Gerald— and from my own rage. I had wanted to hit him, punch him until his fat nose bled all over his fat stupid face. *Yes.* What could he have done about it that he hadn't already done? What was left?

Last night at dinner, Gerald had told me that I had no respect for family values.

"What does destroying the heron's nest have to do with family values?" I had shouted back at him. "You'll be in a lot of trouble now, and it serves you right."

Gerald's face swelled. "That nest...that tree...everything on the hill belongs to me and the tabernacle! You betrayed your own kin when you told that boy about the nest and he told his father...the crazy tree-hugger! My God in heaven, what has this world come to! I told you to stay away from those people, and you betrayed me and they turned me over to the government. You did this, Jocelyn. You made me cut down the tree. It's your fault. I try to be a father to you..."

"I have a father!" I shouted.

"And he left you to me to raise, but you defy me and betray me and hand me over to my enemies!"

He had followed me to my bedroom door, and I slammed it in his face and closed the bolt I had installed myself.

"Open this door!" he shouted. "Nobody locks a door on me in my own house! I'll kick it down if you don't open it right now!"

"Jocelyn, please!" my half-sister, Hope, cried. "Please stop this!"

And so I slid back the bolt and opened the door. Gerald was gasping, one hand pressed to his chest. His pale blue eyes bulged in his face.

"Never..." he began as he lurched toward me. "You never..."

"You stay away from me!" I yelled.

"Stop this!" Hope cried. "Jocelyn, how can you? You know I'm leaving tomorrow, and you act like this. I need to go on this retreat! Where's your gratitude? What would Dad say if he knew how you treat us?"

I didn't answer, but I thought that Dad would say what he always said. Don't make things hard for your sister. Poor Hope, he'd say. She's never been as strong as you, and she has all these problems, what with the two boys being such brats and Gerald so selfish and overbearing.

I'd wanted to call Dad in Berlin the night before so he wouldn't worry when he heard I'd run off, but he would have told Hope so she could stop me, and I couldn't risk it.

I decided I'd call Dad the first time the bus stopped. By then he might already know I'd run away. But no. Hope wouldn't call him until she had tried my friends first.

My friends didn't know anything—I wasn't allowed to talk to them anymore—so what could they say? June would cry and Penny would start out on her bike to look in all our favorite places. And Baily's parents would say he'd gone to the ocean with Gary's family, so he couldn't know anything about me.

But sooner or later Hope and Gerald would talk to Dad. "The girl's impossible, that's all," Gerald would say. "Can you imagine running away because somebody cut down a tree? Don't say I didn't warn you what would happen if you didn't give us more control over her."

The air conditioner on the bus didn't seem to be working. I was sorry I'd worn jeans—I should have known they'd be too hot. The knit shirt hadn't been a great idea, either. Two passengers sitting in the center of the bus complained loudly to the driver, who didn't answer. Baily stood up, pulled his sweatshirt off, and jammed it into the overhead. His T-shirt was blue, like his eyes.

I brushed my light brown bangs off my damp forehead. I'd had my hair cut very short a week before and at first I'd been sorry. But now I was glad. Short hair was easier to take care of at the lake, where there wasn't any hot water for shampoos unless you heated it over a fire.

The bus pulled into the small brick depot in Riverford. "All passengers off," the driver said crossly, as if we'd behaved badly somehow. "We'll be here half an hour."

"I want to stay on the bus," the old woman with the book called out. "I always stay on."

"I'm taking the bus to the garage to check the air conditioning unit," the driver said. "Everybody off."

Baily and I waited until most of the others had crowded into the aisle before we stood up. A girl in a bright red shirt, last in line, looked back at Baily and smiled. She was about our age, I guessed—fifteen. Baily didn't notice, but then he never did. He pawed at his thick dark hair and sighed, waiting his turn.

Inside the depot, he headed for the men's room and I stopped at the first phone I saw and I dug out the telephone calling card Dad had given me. I had memorized his number in Germany, and that long line of figures, along with the ones on the card, worried me. I always expected to make a mistake. I punched out numbers carefully and waited. In Berlin, Dad's home phone rang and rang. At last his answering machine clicked on with a beep and a moment of ear-splitting electronic feedback. "Charles Tyler can be reached in Rome," Dad's calm voice said. He gave another long number and the tape ended. He hadn't asked for messages.

I hung up. In his last call, Dad had told me he'd leave for Rome on Sunday. This was Friday, so that meant he probably was spending the weekend with friends again.

And I didn't remember the number he'd given on the answering machine.

I'd call back and write the number down, just in case Dad had gone straight to Rome. But I didn't have a pencil! What was wrong with me? Maybe Baily had a pen or pencil. I'd ask as soon as I saw him.

But maybe it was just as well I didn't talk to Dad now. I might not be able to keep from telling him where I was going. Dad would call Hope, because Hope was my guardian when Dad was in Europe. And Hope would tell Gerald—who had been appointed by God, he said, to be head of the family.

I put the phone card away and made my way through the crowd toward the lunch counter. I hadn't eaten since dinner the night before, and I hadn't finished that meal because Gerald had taken so long saying the blessing that the pork grease on the platter had congealed into thick white circles. Maybe I could think better now if I had something in my stomach.

All the seats at the counter were filled, but a few people were ordering sandwiches at the cash register, so I did, too. The woman with the book had coffee, and smiled at me when she tasted it.

"Not too horrible," she said.

Baily ordered a hamburger, and was told it would take several minutes. I had asked for a cheese sandwich and orange juice, but the man taking orders forgot the juice. I didn't complain because I didn't want to draw attention to myself, so I took the sandwich outside and ate alone beside the building in a dusty strip of shade.

Two young men from the bus stopped beside me. I ignored them, but the one in the baseball cap said, "Hi," anyway. I didn't answer.

"Where are you going?" the other one asked. "All the way to Idaho?"

"No," I said, and regretted even that small truth.

"Where are you getting off, then?" the first one asked.

"My dad's meeting me at Price River," I lied. Price River was one stop past where I was going.

"You live there?" the second one asked.

"Yes," I said. "Excuse me. I want a magazine."

I walked away from them briskly, but my heart was hammering. I hated lying. And I wasn't very good at it.

Baily turned pages in a magazine while he ate his hamburger. I passed him, scowling, and sat on a bench next to the woman with the book. She didn't look up. Baily shrugged, and I knew by his expression that he wouldn't go back to Seattle without a lot of persuading.

In half an hour, the passengers returned to the bus bay, but the bus wasn't there. We waited for ten minutes, fifteen. A short, stocky man marched inside and came back with the news that the bus would start loading in five minutes. Baily said he needed a drink of water and disappeared.

"I don't remember seeing you in Price River."

The young man again. He had startled me and I jerked away from him. He laughed and followed, his friend slouching beside him.

"We've been there," his friend said. "How come we

didn't notice a girl with eyes like yours? What are they—
blue? Gray?"

"Maybe you didn't notice her because she's young
enough to be your daughter," the woman with the book
snapped. She pushed between me and the man wearing
the baseball cap and elbowed him sharply. "Excuse me,"
she said. "You're standing in my place. You'll have to go
somewhere else."

The two men moved off, red-faced, laughing a little.

"Thanks," I said.

"Bus travel isn't what it used to be," the woman said.

"I guess," I said. This was the first time I'd taken the
bus to the lake alone. Grandma and Gran-auntie hated to
drive, so after Grandpa died, we took the bus. But our last
trip to the lake had been two years ago, and I couldn't
remember much about the journey, probably because it
had been so carefully planned that nothing unusual had
happened. Grandma and Gran-auntie always arranged
everything down to the smallest detail so they could stay
in control. I liked that. If nothing was left to chance, then
there weren't many ways things could go wrong.

"Of course," the old woman said, "nothing's what it
used to be." She laughed and shook her head. Her silver
earrings jingled. "Or what it ought to be."

She was right, I thought. Pain engulfed me suddenly.
Everything had changed after Grandma died and
Gran-auntie moved into the retirement home. When
chaos replaced order.

The bus came, but the air conditioning still didn't
work. The driver said repairs would be made at the next

stop, Franklin Springs. I would leave the bus there.

The heat was awful. Passengers fanned themselves with anything handy and complained for miles, until at last, exhausted, they gave up. I closed my burning eyes.

Maybe I should have borrowed a pencil and called Germany again to get Dad's number in Rome. It was nearly noon—it would be night in Italy. If I'd found him, I could have told him nothing except that I was all right and he wasn't to worry about me. But then, Gran-auntie might have contacted him already, unless he was with friends.

I'd told Dad before—*But why hadn't he listened?*—that I hated Gerald, that I couldn't stand being in the same house with him. All Dad had said was, "I'll be back by Christmas, and we'll sort everything out then. Don't make things hard for your sister."

So what could I say now? I would need a better story than what happened with the tree and the heron's nest. Dad wouldn't understand that what Gerald had done to punish me for standing up to him had been the last straw—unless I told everything else. And I couldn't. And Gerald could be counted on to make everything I said sound ridiculous. To make me sound crazy—or dishonest. He always did that to anyone he quarrelled with. And self-centered Hope would back him up because that was the easy way out.

I was too hot to think. Later, at the lake, I'd decide what to do. Right now it was enough to know that I had taken the first steps to rescue myself.

The bus pulled into the Franklin Springs depot and the passengers crowded forward to the door. "We're leaving in half an hour," the driver called out.

"Oh, sure," the old woman with the book scoffed.

I waited until nearly everyone had left the bus before I pulled my duffel bag out from under the seat.

"I'm getting off," I told Baily. "You can take a bus back to Seattle."

I hurried inside to the women's lounge, locked myself in a booth, and changed into a thin yellow shirt and dark blue shorts. After I stuffed my heavy clothes into the duffel bag, I slung the strap over my shoulder and left. I looked straight ahead to the door, hoping Baily didn't see me.

After Grandpa died, Grandma hired someone to drive us the two miles to the cabin. I could walk that far, no matter how hot it was, because at the end of the walk waited the lake. If I concentrated on that, the sun wouldn't bother me.

I kept my head down, hoping no one would remember me and wonder what I was doing there. I crossed the street and headed east, to Ridge Loop Road. The duffel bag seemed to get heavier with every step I took. I switched it to my other shoulder and then back again. When I passed the last house, I ran out of sidewalk, but then there was less chance of being recognized.

The road shoulders were rough gravel, overgrown with blackberry vines bearing dusty, sweet-scented fruit, so I walked on the asphalt most of the time. On the left, clear-cut land stretched north for many scorched and ugly miles. I couldn't bear to look at the devastation.

On the right, second-growth evergreens hissed in the

hot wind. No cars passed me going in either direction. The only company I had was a crow flying overhead and occasionally hurling curses down at me.

I sensed someone walking behind me before I heard him. Baily. He had a knapsack on his back, with my jacket and his sweatshirt bundled under one arm.

"You forgot your jacket," he said when he drew close enough for me to hear him. "You aren't very good at running away."

"I don't want you following me," I said.

"I'm bringing you your jacket," he said with an annoying show of patience. He handed it to me. "Do you know where you're going? It doesn't look like there's anything on this road for miles."

"I know exactly where I'm going," I said. "Did you ask about getting a bus back to Seattle?"

"There are lots of buses," he said.

I began walking again, a little faster now, the duffel bag strap cutting into my shoulder.

We passed between the clear-cut land and a broken, rocky ridge, lightly shaded by stunted old evergreen trees. I recognized with relief the halfway landmark, the four-foot-high granite boulder with a huckleberry bush growing out of a wide crack in the top.

"I'm turning off pretty soon," I told Baily. "I don't want you coming along. I know you mean well, but you're only complicating things."

"What things?" he said.

"Well, if Gerald should find me..." I began.

"You could stay with my parents," he said. "You could explain about Gerald..."

"I'm not telling anybody anything!" I shouted at him, instantly angry. "Will you get that through your head?"

I walked away from him, too upset to talk anymore. If Baily knew everything, I thought, he wouldn't want me to tell his parents. What would his family think about me? My own sister was married to Gerald and *knew* about him and still blamed me for what he did.

Baily's parents would blame me too, and not want Baily to be my friend. Not that it mattered. I didn't need him anyway.

"Get away from me, Baily," I said. "Just leave me alone."

"Can't," he said. "You don't know what you're doing."

$\mathcal{T}$ W O

$\mathcal{E}$xasperated, I stopped and waited for Baily to catch up with me. The sun poured down on me, cooking me.

"You just won't listen, will you?" I said when he got close enough to hear me.

"Nope," he said. He didn't smile—he rarely did.

"I can't stand here arguing with you," I said. "Cars hardly ever come by, but I don't want anyone from town seeing me. We knew lots of people there, and I'm sure they've heard my grandparents died. They'd wonder what I'm doing here, and maybe even get in touch with the care-taker."

"Give me that," Baily said as he grabbed my duffel bag away from me and slung it over his shoulder. "Would he call your sister? The caretaker, I mean. Does he live around here?"

"It's a she. Justine Poe. She moved away and stopped working for us, but she had lots of friends in town and if she heard anything, she'd come back here to see what's going on." Justine, the tall black woman who had been cranky with everyone except Grandma and Gran-auntie, was one of those people who takes charge, straightens things out, gets to the bottom of everything. I grinned, remembering Justine. But as much as I had liked her, I didn't want her showing up and asking me questions.

"But would she get in touch with Hope?" Baily asked.

"No, I don't think so. I doubt if she would have her phone number."

Whom could Justine tell about seeing me? Grandma was dead, and Gran-auntie had moved to a retirement home in San Francisco. Justine wouldn't know about that or have her new telephone number. She didn't know Hope, because Hope wasn't *family*. She and I had different mothers and maternal grandparents. Hope had visited us at the lake only once, and the day had been such a disaster that she was never invited again, thanks to Gerald, who had spoiled the picnic supper by inflicting on us a rambling and pompous blessing that managed to insult everyone at the table except himself. No, there was no one for Justine to tell.

But still, it was better not to stir things up.

"You said your aunt knows you're going to stay here," Baily said. "She thought it was all right? You being here alone a million miles from anywhere?"

"She hated the idea, especially since she hasn't been able to find anybody to take care of the place," I said. "But that just worked out better for me. If nobody sees me, nobody can talk about me. Here, we turn off the road now. See?"

"So why did she let you do it?"

"How could she stop me?" I said. "She wanted me to check into a hotel until she figured out what to do. She said she'd call and make a reservation for me, but the people in the hotel might have thought that was really strange—me staying there all alone. So I said I'd come here."

"Couldn't she have come to Seattle to get you?"

"She just got out of the hospital," I said.

Baily sighed. "This is crazy," he said. "There must have been a better way of doing all this."

"It's none of your business," I said.

The road we walked along was not much more than a grassy track with thick brush intruding on it. Grandpa couldn't have driven a car to the cabin any longer. The road rose a little to the ridge, and then plunged through woods. I strode in knee-high grass and wildflowers, and the birds in the trees fell silent as I passed. I suspected that my misery clanged around me like broken, discordant bells.

Baily followed doggedly. His footsteps were quieter than mine, padding gently while I crashed and stumbled. I was afraid he was not even leaving a trail through the tall grass. His ease with the surroundings—*my* surroundings—infuriated me.

"I don't know, Jocelyn," he said. "I don't think this is a good idea."

I stopped. "There was no other way, none! I'm doing the only thing I can. Now if you don't like it, you can leave. I didn't want you here anyway."

Baily only looked at me. His damp, dark hair curled

over his forehead and his skin was so deeply tanned that his eyes seemed to gleam. He looked taller. This was Baily, my silent shadow in the high school halls? I had a sudden feeling that he could read my mind.

I hurried along the track again, my fists clenched. Ahead, I saw light streaming at a slant through the trees. Beyond, the cabin lay in a broad, shallow depression that Grandpa said had been scooped out by a glacier thousands of years ago.

I looked back. "Your parents will be mad when they find out where you spent the weekend," I said.

He caught up with me. "Come on," he said. "Let's see if anybody's here."

"Nobody's here," I said.

"A tramp might have broken in. And sometimes hikers break into places."

"I'm sure no one broke into the cabin," I said. He walked quickly, forcing me to run to keep up. "No one ever has. Anybody can see through the windows that nothing in the place is worth stealing."

"Sure," he said.

I hated his overbearing attitude. Hadn't I ever noticed that about him before? I was in no mood to let someone else take control of the situation.

And I would have given anything to have his self-confidence. From the way he acted, anybody might think Baily ran away every month of the year.

"So you talked this old lady into letting you come out here by yourself," Baily said. "It doesn't sound as if she understands that it could be dangerous."

"Are you saying she's senile or doesn't care about me?" I demanded. "She was very worried. But I told her I'd walk into town and call her as often as she liked, only she thought I might be recognized if I kept running back and forth. So we worked it out that I'd only go there once to call, on Monday at two o'clock exactly."

"That's three days away," Baily said.

"She'll need time to find Dad. She's going to ask him to fax her something that makes her my guardian. And she'll call my old school in San Francisco to make arrangements for me to go back as a boarding student."

"Still, staying in a hotel would have been better than this," Baily said.

"Gerald and Hope could have found me in a hotel in Seattle," I told Baily. "I didn't want to take the chance. But they'd never look for me here."

We left the trees behind, and the great green hollow spread out before us, cupping the sunlight. The brightness was almost audible. The lake lay flat and serene, reflecting the white-streaked sky. On the island in the center, the willow tree Grandpa had planted when he was young spread out its great, gnarled branches. Two Canada geese floated, dozing, among a flock of ducks near the reeds.

The square white cabin sat at the water's edge, surrounded on all sides by a shabby, peeling porch, supported on pilings. The cook shack, nothing more than a vine-covered arbor built around an outdoor fireplace with a stovetop, a sturdy table, and a stone sink with a well pump, stood farther up the slope, safely out of the water's reach even in flood time. Two hundred feet away, a windowless storage shed served as support for climbing scarlet roses. Behind it, an outhouse was covered with roses and a rough tangle of honeysuckle.

Baily glanced briefly at the padlock on the door of the storage shed as he passed and then tramped to the cabin. The door there was padlocked, also. "It doesn't look like anybody's been here," he said.

I pulled out the key that I kept on a string around my neck, but I couldn't turn it in the rusted padlock. Baily tried several times before he finally succeeded. He handed me the padlock and key, and then pushed open the door.

The air inside the one-room cabin was stifling. A layer of dust covered the wood plank floor, and long, elaborate cobwebs drifted like veils from the ceiling.

"There's no furniture except for that table and a couple of chairs," Baily said. "How can you stay here? There isn't even a bed."

"The cabin's got everything I need," I said. "Thanks for opening the door, but you don't need to stay. You should head back to Seattle now."

"It gets cold at night in places like this, but I don't see any wood for the stove. And what about food? The nearest grocery store is clear back in town." Baily acted as if he hadn't heard me tell him to leave.

"Go home. I'll be fine." I picked up my bag and stepped inside.

"You didn't remember to bring a sleeping bag, either," he said.

My head throbbed. Miserable and scared, I needed time alone to think, and Baily wasn't giving it to me. I cov-

ered my eyes with my hands for a moment, sighed, and
said, "I don't want you here, and I'm not going to let you
stay. I can take care of myself. Just get out and go home. I
mean it."

"Okay, okay!" Baily growled. "Suit yourself."

He turned to leave and I shut the door behind him.
It bounced open and I slammed it.

Each cabin wall had a row of windows. I watched
Baily first through the windows closest to the door and
then through the south windows. He'd better not come
back!

When he was out of sight, I opened the window seat
closest to me and tugged out a cushion, made to fit the
seat.

"Here's my bed!" I said aloud, as if he were still there,
watching me. I took several blankets out of the window
seat and shook them out of their plastic coverings. Next
came sheets and pillows, and a red plaid bedspread.

The window seat on the east wall contained more
bedding, a box of dishes, and an assortment of pans.
Across the room, the window seats did not lift up. Panels
under each one slid back to reveal canned food, candles, a
silver candelabra wrapped in plastic, a first-aid kit, several
flashlights and electric lanterns, and a shoebox filled with
batteries.

"They're dead by now, I bet," I muttered. I remembered what Grandma always did first when we reached the
cabin, and I put batteries in one of the lanterns. It worked!
Now I could find my way to the outhouse after dark.
Grandma had taught me to leave nothing to chance.

Another cupboard contained towels, dozens of them, faded and limp but clean; and an assortment of old swimsuits, T-shirts and sweatshirts, jeans and shorts, socks and pajamas, in many sizes.

I sat on the window seat and looked around. Late afternoon light streamed through the uncurtained windows, illuminating the dust. There was a mop in the storage shed. But it was so hot, and the cool lake waited outside.

I pulled my swimsuit from my bag, stripped off my clothes, and changed. Then I unlatched the French door, the one that led to the part of the porch that overhung the water.

The porch creaked under my weight, reminding me that Grandmother had planned to have someone replace the pilings under it. But it was safe enough for one person. I sat on the railing, swung my legs over, and splashed into the lake.

The water came to my chin. Ripples rocked lily pads close to the cabin and then spread out near the ducks, who squawked a little and watched me curiously. The geese, too elegant to share the water with a clumsy human, paddled off to the far end where the lake emptied quietly into a wide stream that eventually fell into a rocky canyon and finally over a waterfall.

I plunged under and came up sputtering, my hair plastered to my head. The ducks protested this behavior and flew off. On the wooded ridge, a crow scolded everything in sight. I ducked again, and then scaled the ladder back to the porch.

For the first time since I climbed out my bedroom window at five thirty that morning, I smiled.

By evening, I had cleaned the cabin and made up one window seat into a bed. The twilight was clear and shadowless, but surprisingly cool. I dug out one of Grandpa's old sweatshirts and draped it over my shoulders.

Then I brought two dozen white candles out to the porch. I set most of them on the railings all around the cabin, but I put the great silver candelabra in the center of the small table on the south side. When all the candles were burning steadily in the still air, I sat at the table, drank a can of tomato juice, and ate a dozen stale crackers. I was too tired to fix a meal.

Twice, just before darkness filled the hollow, a loon called out. "Make a wish," Grandmother would have said each time.

I wish Dad would come home from Europe early and we could go back to San Francisco to live together.

Is that two wishes or only one? I wondered.

To be safe, I would wait until the loon called again. But he didn't, and after a while a weak, cold wind fluttered the candle flames. Any hope of magic that night was gone. I blew out all the candles except those in the candelabra.

I was alone in the dark. But I was safer at the cabin than in the same house with Gerald. If I'd stayed in Seattle, I would have been alone with him and his two young sons for ten long days, while Hope was away at her church retreat. Ten days of quarrels and threats. Ten days of being on guard. I wasn't sure if I still had the strength for it. Not anymore. Not since Gerald had cut down the tree.

It was my fault. If I had only kept the heron a secret, then Baily's father wouldn't have told the county wildlife people about it, and Gerald would never have heard about it. I had wanted to hurt Gerald, but I had only succeeded in giving him a weapon to use on me. And one bird had died. All my fault.

I brought the candelabra inside and put it on a windowsill, then wrapped myself in a blanket and curled up on my bed. It was cold enough for a fire in the stove, and I'd brought kindling and split logs down from the cook shack. But I was too tired to make the effort. When the candles burned out, I'd crawl under my blankets. I knew I'd sleep well.

Someone knocked on the door. I froze. Who could it be? Should I call out? Pretend I wasn't alone?

"Jocelyn," I heard.

It was Baily. I leaped up and ran to the door.

"You again?" I cried. "You were supposed to go back to Seattle."

"I brought you something to eat. It's not a lot, but it's better than going hungry."

"I'm not hungry," I said. "I've got plenty of canned things to eat."

Baily was silent for a moment, and then he said, "Can you lock this door from the inside?"

I gaped at him. "What? Lock it? I don't know. Nobody ever locks it when we're here."

He sighed. "Well, look at the door, for crying out loud. Is there a deadbolt or something? You shouldn't be out here by yourself in a place without a lock on the inside."

I fumbled around the doorknob. "I don't know—I don't think there's anything like a deadbolt."

"Reach up higher—here, let me do it." Baily pushed open the door. "That's what I thought. There's nothing. You have to do something to protect yourself."

"Who am I supposed to be afraid of?" I cried. "You're the only other person I've seen around here."

"Jocelyn, I'm trying to help."

"Well, you *aren't* helping. You're giving me things to worry about that never crossed my mind before. Now go home, before I get really mad."

He laughed suddenly, and in the lantern's glare, I saw that the laughter had transformed his face. The Baily I had always thought of as a solitary, lonely dragon had been caught off guard.

"You might scare Gerald but you don't scare me," he said. "Don't you want the sandwiches? They're roast beef."

I hesitated and sighed. "I'll split them with you," I said. "We can sit at the table on the porch."

I carried the lantern out and he followed me. The porch shook a little under our feet, but Baily didn't say anything. He emptied a paper sack out on the table and pushed a plastic-wrapped sandwich and a can of root beer toward me.

"The sandwich looks almost as good as homemade," I said. "Where did you get it?"

"From the deli in town," he said. "They didn't ask questions and I didn't say anything."

We ate in silence, and when we were done, I gathered up the cans and plastic bags. "Thanks for the meal," I said.

"I guess I was hungrier than I thought. I've got plenty of food here, but ..." I was talking too much, I knew. I got to my feet and picked up the lantern. "It was a long walk for you. I'm sorry about all the trouble you went to."

"No trouble, Jocelyn."

"But you still can't stay here."

He looked away from me, toward the cook shack. "I could stay there."

"There's no roof," I said.

"It's not going to rain."

I shook my head. "You're really a big pain. Okay. There's a sleeping bag here that I'll let you use, but only for tonight, and only because it's so late. Tomorrow you leave. Okay?"

While I dragged the sleeping bag out of a cupboard, I realized that he hadn't agreed to leave the next day. But it was too late to go on arguing with him. I shoved the sleeping bag at him.

"Good night," I said.

Sunlight woke me early. I opened the door, stretched, and finger-combed my rumpled hair. A light wind ruffled the surface of the lake and tossed the willow branches. Birds sang and called from all sides, and near the island a goose honked dolefully. Another, out of sight, answered, sounding equally morose.

I filled a bucket with lake water and carried it to the cook shack to prime the old pump there. The lake water was probably safe, but Grandma had insisted we drink well water. It seemed important to me to do everything the way Grandma would. In an unsettled time like this, it was best to move steadily and surely on all the familiar paths.

Baily sat at the rough wood table in the cook shack, whittling on a stick. He looked up, faintly scowling.

"If you'd got up a half hour earlier," he said, as if he had reason to expect more of me, "you'd have seen the deer wading in the lake."

Baily the dragon was back. I put down the bucket. "I bet you're sorry you stayed here last night," I said.

"Let's face it," he said. "It was too far to go home in the dark."

I suspected that traveling long distances in the dark didn't bother Baily at all. I didn't really know him. It wasn't easy to understand people you rarely saw outside school, and Baily was especially solitary. That I knew him even a little was because of the heron I'd mentioned in class once. He'd wanted to see the nest and I'd walked there with him after school.

And, of course, after his father started the trouble with the wildlife people, Baily and I had met a few times secretly in the park to exchange news. So perhaps I did know him as well as anyone could.

"Who's Annie?" Baily asked.

I flinched. "What?"

He pointed to one of the arbor's supporting posts, the one Grandma had marked with my height each summer. My name had been carved above the marks, and my birth-date. On the other side of the post was my mother's name, Annie, and all her marks. The carving there was darker and heavily weathered.

"Who is she?" Baily asked.

"My mother," I said.

"Sorry," Baily said. "I remember you told me she died when you were born, so you lived with your grandparents. I knew things were hard for you the first time I saw you at school. You kept to yourself so much. I liked that. You sort of drifted around in the background."

"Like you," I said quickly, interrupting him. I knew where he was heading, and I didn't want to hear any more about how I should tell people the truth about Gerald. As if Baily could even guess the whole truth.

"No, not like me," Baily said. He sighed and shrugged. "Now you're going away, and just about the only thing we ever talked about was the heron's nest."

That's true, I thought. But somehow, in those conversations, we had learned that we were alike.

"I'll be leaving on Monday," I said to remind him, and he looked away, toward the lake.

"I know," he said. He sighed again.

THREE

Baily helped me prime the pump in the cook shack, and then pumped water until both of us were satisfied it was clean enough to drink.

"What are you going to eat for breakfast?" Baily asked me as he carried the empty bucket back to the cabin for me.

"I've got lots of things—canned fruit and even canned brown bread. I've got powdered orange juice, too. And foil packages of nuts and things, but I don't like those."

Baily shook his head in disgust. "Why didn't you stop at the store before you walked out here?"

"I forgot," I lied, doing my best to sound indifferent. I'd been afraid someone in the store would remember me. I jumped up on the porch ahead of him and shoved the door open.

"I could go in town and pick up something for us," Baily said.

For us? He was taking a lot for granted.

Suddenly I wasn't sure I could trust him. It occurred to me that he might take it upon himself to get in touch with his parents and tell them about me. I had no idea how they would react, but this was not a situation I could risk. I'd better keep Baily here, I thought, because as long as he's with me, he won't be back in town phoning his parents about me.

Also, Hope and Gerald might have told the police by now, and I didn't know how authorities went about looking for missing kids. Would all the police in the state already know about me? If someone found out I was here, would I be dragged back to Gerald before Gran-auntie could make plans to get me home to California where I belonged? What would Gerald do to me then?

"Put the bucket on the table," I told Baily. I added, "Please," after he turned his bright eyes toward me indignantly.

He set the bucket down and then rubbed his hands against his shirt. I was certain it was a nervous gesture, and I felt better knowing he wasn't as self-assured as he liked to pretend.

"Well?" he asked, avoiding looking straight at me. "Should I go in town and get us something that isn't canned?"

"There's nothing wrong with canned food," I said.

"Yes, but how long has it been here?" he asked. "Since last year? Is that when you were here before?"

"I was here two years ago," I said.

"I don't want to eat anything that was canned that long ago," he said.

I pulled a can of peaches and a jar of powdered orange juice out of the cupboard. "Okay," I said. "But this is what's for breakfast."

I set two places at the table on the porch, and he joined me while I spooned peaches into both bowls. We ate in silence, watching the ducks and geese float near the island. Time had stopped here, the way it always did. It was impossible to imagine any form of danger in this place.

"Sometimes we ate breakfast in the rowboat," I said. "Once, even when it was raining."

"Where's the boat?"

"In the storage shed. I'll get it out when we're done. I hope it's still all right."

When we went to look, we found the old rowboat in good condition, but Baily said the only way of telling for certain was to put it in the water. We skidded it down the slope to the edge of the lake and shoved it out into the reeds. I took off my shoes, waded in after the boat, and boosted myself up over the side.

"I don't see any water leaking in," I reported.

"Boats usually wait to leak until you're out in the middle of a lake," Baily said. "I think it's some sort of rule, like only getting a flat tire when it's raining. Let's try the boat out before we trust it."

I took the seat in the center and fitted the oars in place. Baily tossed his shoes in the direction of the porch and pushed the boat out to clear water, then crawled into the stern. His clothes were wet to his chest.

"You haven't anything else to wear," I said as I dipped the oars in the water.

"No," Baily said. He looked away as if I had embarrassed him.

There were clothes in the cabin that might fit him, but I wouldn't offer them to him because he'd assume I wanted him to stay.

But then, he could make trouble for me if he left and told anyone about me.

I rowed halfway out to the island and rested on the oars. Beyond the sloping meadow, the stunted trees on the rocky ridge looked more formidable than they actually were, presenting a barrier between me and the devastation across the road where the parched, clear-cut land rolled north. A hawk dipped and circled over the meadow, then plunged to earth. I looked away quickly. Hawks had to eat. Everything had to survive. But it was better not knowing anything specific about that survival. *Knowing* was always terrible.

I dipped one oar and turned the boat so I faced the island. Here and there on the drooping willow, gold leaves showed. Fall came earlier here. By the time my grandparents, my great-aunt, and I had left for San Francisco at the end of each August, the woods showed bright color everywhere. The sight always had made me sad, even though I had believed I would always return the next year.

I had been so safe in those days. Everything was well ordered and predictable. But mostly, everything had been safe.

The still lake mirrored the sky perfectly, and the boat seemed to be suspended between them. The hawk was back, hanging silently overhead. Nothing ever changed here. My first memory of the lake was the same as the scene around me. In a moment, Grandma might step out of the cook shack, cup her hands, and shout to us that lunch was ready.

Suddenly rings of ripples slapped the side of the boat, and the sky in the water tore apart. A goose sailed out from under an overhanging willow branch and honked indignantly, as if we had been responsible for the disturbance.

I glanced at Baily, expecting to see him grin, but he was looking toward the horizon, his expression sober. He seemed lost somehow, and achingly sad.

"Are you running away, too?" I blurted.

He looked up and hesitated before answering. His eyes flickered, and then he said, "No. I don't do that anymore."

"You lie to your parents instead," I said.

"I guess."

I dug the oars into the water and moved the boat. Without speaking again, I rowed to the eastern end of the lake, to the narrow passage that separated it from another lake out of sight behind the trees, and still another lake beyond that one.

"What's there?" Baily asked.

"Two other lakes," I said. "The one farthest away used to have a small hotel on it, but it burned down the winter after the forest was clear-cut. People say the man who owned it set fire to it because the woods were gone and everything was so ugly."

"What's in the other direction?" he asked.

"A creek and then a waterfall," I said. "After that, I don't know. Grandpa and I never walked that far."

Baily nodded, satisfied.

I rowed around the island, out of sight of the cabin. On the far side, a small current in the lake moved the boat. I rested on the oars again and we drifted to the other end of the island.

"Who's that?" Baily asked suddenly, softly.

I looked in the direction he pointed, and saw someone galloping down the slope from the woods, heading toward the cabin.

It was a black boy, perhaps thirteen, I guessed, skinny and knobby-kneed, dressed in baggy blue shorts and a big flapping black T-shirt. A black cap covered his head. He had a bulging pack and a sleeping bag on his back and swung a plastic grocery bag.

"He acts as if he knows where he's going," Baily said, and he didn't sound pleased.

The newcomer hopped clumsily up on the porch and disappeared inside the cabin.

"Hey!" I yelled immediately. I rowed toward the cabin, splashing water. "Hey, you!" I shouted over my shoulder. "You get out of that cabin!"

The stranger appeared immediately on the porch without his bags and stood there while I rowed closer.

"You, what do you think you're doing?" I shouted. "Stay out of my house!"

The boy pulled off his cap and held it to his chest. His hair was straight and pulled tightly back into a ponytail.

"Is this your place?" he shouted across the water.

I pulled harder on the oars. "What do you want?" I shouted. I bumped the boat into the porch and tied the boat's frazzled line to a post.

"Now!" I said when I climbed the ladder. "Answer me! What do you want?"

The boy, no taller than I, backed up a step. But he didn't answer.

"Who are you?" I demanded. "Tell me."

He pulled his hat back on and grinned nervously. "You can call me Spider," he said. "Or Ugly. I answer to anything."

"What are you doing here?" I asked.

The stranger shrugged. "Nothing. Just looking around, sort of. How about you?"

"I own this place," I said.

The boy stared and then grinned. "No kidding? But let's say you don't own it. How come you're here?"

Baily jumped over the railing and advanced on him. "We asked first," he said.

The stranger batted his long nose nervously. "If I answer, will you?"

Baily grabbed his shoulders and pulled him close. "I'll count to three and you better answer. *Three!*"

"Ow!" the boy screeched. "You cheated! Don't hit me!"

Baily let go of him. "I didn't hit you, not yet. But you better start talking."

"I come here all the time," the stranger babbled. "Nobody's ever here! I didn't think anybody cared."

"I care, so get out," I said. "Where's your stuff? Did you leave it inside? Get it and get out of here."

The boy darted inside and dragged out his belongings. "So I guess this means we can't be friends," he said. "Is that what you're telling me? Because if that's how it's going to be, then you don't care if I tell anybody you're here. I could mention to the sheriff in Franklin Springs that this boy and girl are shacked up..."

"What?" I yelled, outraged. I flew at him and might have slapped him if he hadn't ducked expertly enough to tell me that he'd been socked more than once in his life.

"Okay, okay," the boy said. "Sorry. Don't get so mad. Look, I can't go back home for a while, at least until my mom finds another job and cheers up. I won't bother you if you don't bother me, okay? There's plenty of room here for all of us."

"You said you came here all the time," I said. "Is your mother always out of a job?"

"Pretty much," he said. "I couldn't have described my situation better myself."

Baily burst out laughing, then sobered instantly.

I glared at him. "You think that's funny?" I said. "He's nothing but a smart-ass, and you think it's funny?"

"Okay, so it's not funny," Baily said. But he was grinning.

The stranger raised his big hand and Baily slapped it, palm to palm. "You're okay," the stranger told Baily.

"I don't believe any of this," I said. "How often did you come here?"

The boy rolled his eyes. "Couple of times?"

"Is that all?"

"Maybe more than that?"

"Well, is it more than that or not? Can't you answer a question instead of asking another one?"

He ducked his head. "Answers get me in trouble. How about you cut me a deal? I can't go home right now. There are problems—insinuations and accusations, if you get my meaning. So maybe you could see your way clear to letting me stay, if I don't get in the way. I brought my own food and I'll sleep outside and not bother you two."

"What?" I cried, outraged again at the implication that Baily and I had some sort of unnamed relationship.

Baily held a restraining hand on my arm. "How old are you?" he asked the boy.

"Old enough," the boy asked.

"He's older than thirteen," I told Baily angrily. "He's got too many smart answers for thirteen."

"If you want to stay alive around my mother, you get smart quick," the boy said. "Look, we got a deal or not? I won't bother you and I won't talk about you if you let me stay a couple days."

What difference would one more person make? Baily didn't seem to be in a hurry to leave. And he wasn't bad company. Actually, I felt better with Baily being there, but I didn't plan on admitting it.

"You have to sleep outside," I told the boy.

The boy smiled and shook his grocery bag. "Sure. And I'll share this with you," he said. "I got cinnamon rolls and strawberries at the deli in town."

My mouth watered immediately.

"Okay," I said. "But you still don't get to sleep in the house."

The stranger jumped up and down and the porch creaked. "I'm not sure that's bad news," he said. "I think this place will sink pretty soon. The *Titanic* is what I'd call it." He handed me the sack. "Is it time for brunch?"

I brought small, unmatched plates out from the cupboard and set the table on the porch. There were only two cinnamon rolls in the sack, but they were twice the size I was accustomed to, so I cut each one in four pieces, gave the boys most of them, and then divided the strawberries equally.

"This is a nice peaceful place," the stranger said as he sat down.

"You ought to know," I said bitterly.

Now there were three of us. Our relationship was delicately balanced, and no matter what reasons the boys had for staying, I believed my reasons were the most serious.

But if Gerald found me here—and now—what would he think? What would he do? Baily and the stranger weren't protection from him. Baily would infuriate him. But the boy, with his glossy black skin and his ponytail...

"There's something nasty about white girls who take up with Negro boys," Gerald had said once when we had seen an interracial couple in a mall.

I had repeated this conversation to my sister. But all Hope had said was, "Leave Gerald alone. You know how he feels about whites mixing up with blacks. Things are bad enough around here already without you thinking up ways to aggravate him."

Goosebumps broke out on my arms. Was the
stranger a bigger threat to me if I threw him out—or let
him stay and risk Gerald's finding us together?

Gerald will never look here, I told myself. Why
would he? No one had mentioned the run-down old summer place for a long time. Gran-auntie was already working out a plan to rescue me from Gerald and Hope. All I
had to do was hang on until Monday.

The stranger popped the last strawberry into his
mouth and looked straight at me. "What are you really
doing here, way out in the middle of nowhere?" he asked.

FOUR

I stood up abruptly. "I don't have to tell you anything," I said. "This is my place, so I'll ask all the questions."

"Hey," the stranger said, protesting, holding up his hands. "I'm only trying to get acquainted, and I sure don't want any trouble. I already told you everything about me."

"No, you didn't," I said. "You said you come here whenever your mom is out of work, but you didn't say why you have to get out of the house then. What's the point in running away?"

"Hoo, listen to her!" he cried. "Doesn't your mother ever get on your back?"

My face burned. I wasn't about to admit to this stranger that my mother was dead.

"So what does your mom do, hit you?" I asked the boy.

"I'd settle for that," he said. "I'd be glad to settle for it." He resettled his cap and looked past me to the lake. "Some things are worse than hitting."

Baily snorted and shook his head. The stranger took that as a challenge and scowled at him.

"Okay," he said. "What does *your* mother do when she's having hard times? Sing and dance? Hand over what's left of her money to you? Call people up and tell them what a great kid you are?"

Baily simply stared at him for a long moment and then sighed.

"I hate this conversation," I said. "Nobody needs to tell anybody anything, because nobody's staying here long enough to care about anybody else."

"Maybe so," the stranger said. "When are you leaving?"

"Monday," I said. "And you won't be staying any longer than that."

"Maybe I need to," he said. "Maybe I'll stay for a while, you know, hang out here and in town, and not bother anybody." He gave me an odd, cold look.

The look worried me, and I wondered if he was goading me. "Go ahead and tell anybody you want that I'm here," I said. "I don't care." I leaned toward him, doing my best to seem as threatening as possible. "I'm not like you. I don't have to worry about my mother hunting me down."

"You got *somebody* hunting you down, don't you?" he said. "Otherwise, why are you here? Why is anybody here?"

I was in dangerous territory. I decided I'd better tell this weird kid something to satisfy him. But how much of the truth could I risk?

"For crying out loud," Baily grumbled. "Are we going to sit here and argue all day?" He got up, stretched, and looked around. "Let's go out in the boat."

My gratitude was mixed with anger. How dare he

take over, as if it was his place to suggest going anywhere in the boat, as if it belonged to him? I was losing control to him, and I couldn't let that go on. But he had succeeded in distracting the newcomer. Had it been a deliberate attempt to help me, or was he only being rude?

"Let's go," I said. "Let's go out to the island for a while and look around."

To make everyone more comfortable, I brought the old canvas boat cushions out from the storage shed. They were striped red and white, but faded now, and marred with rust stains. Still, they reminded me of my childhood, when Grandma would put the cushions on the bottom of the boat so I could nap there, rocking gently. Safe.

Baily rowed that time. I sat in the stern, and the newcomer stood on the small seat in the bow, fists on his bony hips, looking around as if he owned everything in sight.

"You're going to fall in," I told him. "Sit down, right now. I don't want to tip over because you're acting like an idiot."

Baily jerked on the oars, and the stranger nearly lost his balance. He sat down, though, perching on the edge of the seat like a skinny, high-strung bird.

The thought amused me. He actually did look like a young bird, gawky and clumsy, with oversized feet and a great sharp blade of a nose.

"How old are you?" I asked him.

He grinned nervously. "Didn't we give up on me? I'm twelve, thirteen, fourteen, something like that."

"And I can call you Ugly or Spider," I said. "I pick Spider, even though you look more like a bird."

"Okay, sure," the boy said. "What's a good name for a bird?"

"Too late," I said. "We'll call you Spider."

"Okay. I always liked that best anyway," he said.

"Spider," Baily said as he rowed. "Shut up. You talk too much."

"Okay, you got it," Spider said. "I don't want to bother anybody."

Baily gave him a dark, warning look, and Spider hunched over and stopped talking, concentrating on his bug-bitten legs instead.

The boat slid under overhanging willow branches and bumped into the island's low bank. A dozen ducks squawked hysterically, fled into the water, and then took flight. Out of sight, a goose honked and hissed.

"Hey, I like this," Spider said as he climbed out of the boat. He danced through the drooping willow branches until he was out of sight. "This is magic," he called out. "It's better than a tree house. It's better…"

A goose hissed and Spider shrieked.

"Leave the goose alone!" I shouted. "It wasn't hurting you."

"He is now!" Spider yelled. He shot back through the curtain of green willow whips. "Is he behind me? Is he following me?" He was holding his side and grimacing.

I laughed. "He pinched you, didn't he? Serves you right."

Spider rolled his eyes toward Baily, who watched him indifferently. "She could have told me that bird is dangerous," he complained.

Baily shrugged and got out of the boat. He tied the rope to a heavy branch and then pushed his own way through the willow whips, whistling softly through his teeth. Somewhere, the furious goose hissed again, then splashed into the water. Baily disappeared.

"He's your boyfriend, right?" Spider asked me. He rubbed his side carefully, wincing.

"Wrong," I said.

"But the two of you are here together," Spider said. He regarded me with his head cocked to one side. "You guys look like a big item to me."

"I'm here with you, too," I said. "But believe me, you will never be my boyfriend."

"My, my," Spider said, making a prissy face. "Who said I'd ever want somebody as white and skinny as you?"

I was tempted to laugh, which I knew Spider expected, and I ignored him instead. I tried to follow Baily through the branches, but he left no trail, and I ended up in the middle of the island where my grandfather had made a seat from an old log. The log had nearly rotted away. I sat on the ground and leaned my elbows on my knees. The willow branches surrounded me. The lake, the cabin, and the distant forest were all invisible. It was a place I had always come when I wanted to withdraw inside myself, but that wasn't possible now. Disjointed thoughts rattled in my mind, sparking a hundred different anxieties.

The boys were trouble. How had I come to be saddled with both of them? I should have driven Baily away. And Spider—he was more than half crazy and potentially a disaster. He talked too much, and asked too many questions. At least Baily was quiet.

But then, maybe that wasn't so good. I had no idea what he was thinking.

Spider crashed through the branches and sat down beside me, panting a little.

"You make too much noise," I said. "Always."

"I been told that plenty of times," he said. "You didn't answer my question. What's that boy doing here if he isn't your boyfriend?"

Was I safer from the problems Spider could create if he thought Baily was my boyfriend? Would he think Baily might hurt him in some way if he made trouble? I couldn't decide, so I scowled and said, "Don't you understand English? I'm not telling you anything."

Spider, busy picking at a scab on his knee, didn't look at me. "But he's got a name, right? And you, too. What am I supposed to call you?"

"You can call me Ugly," I said.

Spider laughed, looking at me sideways from under his cap. "Ugly, you ain't. But okay, I get your point. My name's really Arnold. Isn't that stupid? Arnold. I hate it, so my friends call me Spider. Now what's your name?"

"Jocelyn," I said, after only the briefest hesitation. My first name couldn't hurt. "The boy's name is Baily."

"Okay!" Spider said, with more enthusiasm than the information deserved. "Now we're getting somewhere. I'm taking a little vacation from home. How about you?"

I glared at him. "Forget it," I said. "How many ways do you have to be told to mind your own business?" I got to my feet and headed back toward the boat.

Trouble. Spider was trouble.

Baily sat in the boat, whittling on a stick. He looked up when I fought my way through the willow branches.

"I'd like to leave that little creep stuck out here," I said as I climbed in the boat with him.

"Suits me," Baily said. "Let's do it." He grabbed the oars.

Spider shot through the branches and tumbled clumsily into the boat with us. "Were you going to leave me out here?" he asked. "You better know right now I can't swim."

"Too bad," I said. I shaded my eyes with my hands and looked toward the place where a crow was screeching across the lake.

It would have been nice to stay out on the water for a while, drifting, resting. But Spider made any sort of rest impossible. He was never still for a moment. Some part of him was always wiggling, twitching, tapping, jiggling. And he couldn't shut up for longer than a minute at a time.

Maybe he'll leave, I thought. I looked up at the bright sky, squinting against the sun. Maybe he'll get bored and take off. Then I'll have peace and quiet.

"What are we going to have for lunch?" Spider asked. "I'm getting hungry again."

Baily helped me make sandwiches out of canned brown bread and ham spread. In the cabin, we found two dozen cans of soft drinks, which weren't cold, but they tasted good, anyway. Spider danced around the table in the cook shack, setting out plates and napkins, humming to himself. Once Baily exchanged a patient look with me, but he didn't say anything. And he didn't smile, either.

In spite of myself, I wondered about Baily. He was so quiet. Was he still wishing I'd talk to his parents about Gerald? It wasn't going to happen. There was no way I'd humiliate myself that way.

But maybe Baily was just being his own quiet self. I'd never been able to decide if he was secretive or so full of self-confidence that he didn't need to babble and fret and worry about what other people thought of him.

Oh, I would have loved being that way, not caring what anyone else thought. What power that would have given me over Gerald these past two years. Then he could have accused me of anything, and I wouldn't have bothered trying to explain myself. My attempts to explain, to justify myself, always ended up providing him with ammunition he used later, either to ridicule me or punish me. Most efforts to stand up to him gave him endless opportunities to twist everything around and make me look like a fool.

Gerald had a hunting lodge in Idaho. During hunting season, he brought home soft-bodied, bloody ducks and quail. And, once, a dead deer lolled in the back of his pickup truck, its abdomen emptied out and yawning.

"God expects a man to provide for his family," he had told me. But that comment didn't explain why he, a preacher, always carried a rifle in his truck, even when he wasn't hunting. He was a bully, and keeping a gun close by was another way of trying to make everybody think he was in charge of everything.

Weeping, I had refused to eat anything he killed, so he wouldn't let me have meat for three months. When he finally realized I didn't care enough about meat to miss it, he told me during dinner that once he had shot a neighbor's cat because he had seen it scratching in his flowerbed. Hope and his young sons went on eating, pretending they didn't hear him. Either what happened to the cat was another of his crazy inventions—Gerald told lies casually—or they had seen him do it and had learned to accept it.

"Why didn't you give the cat to Hope to fix for dinner?" I had said bitterly.

"How do you know I didn't?" Gerald said, and he laughed and laughed when I gagged. For several days he repeated our conversation to everyone, laughing each time.

I hated him. I hated him so much that it made me shake all over sometimes.

"What's wrong?" Spider asked. "You look like you just saw something slimy in the food."

I sat down at my place and pulled the sandwich plate toward me. "Maybe I did," I said. "You'll have to wait and find out." I took two sandwiches and shoved the plate to the center of the table.

Baily helped himself to three sandwiches and shoved the plate to Spider.

"I wish we had potato chips," Spider said as he pried two bread slices apart to examine what was between them. "I don't like sandwiches unless I have potato chips. The chips make the meal, that's what I say. Potato chips or French fries, either one. I don't care which." He slapped the bread together and took a huge bite.

"Will you please shut up?" Baily said.

Spider shrugged. "Okay, okay. But maybe I'll go to town and get some potato chips for us before dinner. How about that? I could pick up other stuff, too. Hamburger or hot dogs, maybe. You name it, I'll bring it back. Does anybody have any money?"

He must not go into town, I decided. He can't stop blabbing. Now that he's here, he has to stay until I leave.

"I don't want hamburger or hot dogs," I said.

"Neither do I," Baily said. "And we don't want anybody running back and forth between here and town, attracting attention. If you're so good at running away, how come you want to hang out where anybody looking for you can find you?"

"Nobody's looking for me," Spider said quickly. "Nobody cares where I go or what happens to me. How about you? Anybody looking for you?"

Baily didn't seem to hear.

"I'll take that as a yes," Spider said. "Somebody's trying to find you. Who?"

"Why do you have to know everything?" I cried. "Can't you mind your own business?"

"I can mind my own business just fine," Spider said, blinking. He took a long drink from his soft drink can, then glared at me resentfully. "But I've been wondering if your parents are the only ones looking for you. Maybe the police are looking for you, too, and that's a whole different bag of trouble. Maybe you did something you shouldn't have done. A big bad something. It's been known to happen."

"We didn't do anything," I said. The sandwiches were good and I was hungry, but Spider had a way of killing my appetite.

"So the two of you *are* together," Spider said. "The two of you *together* didn't do anything. Have I got it straight now?"

I looked up at him and caught his unblinking stare. There was something behind his dark eyes, a kind of curiosity that went far beyond the questions he was asking. Or was it anger I saw? No, of course not. What could he be angry about? He was just one of those people who pries into everything.

Which was safest? Letting him think Baily and I were an involved couple or trying to convince him that we didn't know each other?

Baily leaned over the table toward Spider. "Listen up, you jerk," he said quietly. "If you ask that question about us again, I'm going to do something to you that hurts."

After lunch, Baily wandered off toward the north end of the lake without bothering to say anything.

Spider fidgeted, paced, and yammered about food and the mosquito bites on his skinny legs until I thought I could have cheerfully thrown him in the lake and held his head under water until he stopped talking. I was almost willing to let him go into town alone, for the sake of the silence his absence would bring.

"I'm going out in the boat by myself," I said. "If you're

planning to stay here, you have to do your share of the work. Clean up the lunch stuff, and put the garbage in that plastic bag. We'll take it with us when we leave."

"Throw the garbage in the lake," Spider said. "What do you care?"

"We take our garbage with us when we leave and put it in a trash barrel in town," I said. "That's how it's done here."

"My, my," Spider said. "Maybe you should have left it all for the maid to clean up. Isn't that the real way you do things?"

"We never had a maid," I said. "We had a caretaker, and we never left a mess for Justine to clean up. We took care of our own garbage and our own cleaning."

I was talking too much. I hurried away from Spider, furious with myself. He knew another name now, Justine's. If he went into the small town and blabbed about Justine and me, somebody might put things together and wonder what the Hallbergs' granddaughter was doing at the cabin, since the Hallbergs were dead and Justine wasn't caretaker for them any longer.

Stop it! I told myself. I was worrying about nothing. If I didn't get a strong grip on myself, I wouldn't last until Monday.

By now, Gran-auntie might have already found a place for me, located Dad, and persuaded him to let me return to San Francisco. But if she hadn't, then there was all day tomorrow, Sunday.

I could call tomorrow and ask her, I thought. If things haven't worked out yet, it'll be all right. If I'm careful, no one will see me. And if everything's already settled, then I can leave early, and I won't worry anymore.

No, I told myself. Do everything the way Gran-auntie wanted it done. We had made careful plans, and if I changed them, anything might go wrong. I'd have to hang on until Monday afternoon at two o'clock, and by that time Gran-auntie would have Dad's permission. She'd said she would ask Dad to fax it to her, so everything would be legal. Let Gerald argue about that!

I looked at my watch. In forty-eight hours, everything would be settled. I might even be at the airport, waiting for a plane. It was almost over.

I spent most of the afternoon in the boat, rocking gently on the shady side of the island, watching Spider clean up the cook shack and then sleep stretched out on the table. Baily appeared and disappeared at the far end of the lake, poking through the reeds and brush, bent on some solitary exploration he probably wouldn't explain if I bothered to ask him later. Could I trust him not to involve his parents? The more people who knew about me, the more chances there were for something to go wrong.

If either of the boys took off, I decided, I would leave, too. But where could I go? Where could I hide until Monday?

I'd think of something. If the worst happened, if either of them left and I was afraid I'd be betrayed, I could hide in the woods for a day or so.

As the sun went down, the ripples on the lake died away and the boat stopped rocking. Somewhere on the

other side of the island, a duck murmured once. The pool
of silence widened until it filled the hollow. I thought for
one ecstatic moment that I saw a heron standing among
the reeds, but it didn't move, and finally I decided I was
imagining it, seeing a heron only because of my haunting
sense of loss and guilt.

If only I hadn't told anyone about the nest. If only I
had told someone about Gerald, someone who could have
helped me. If only.

I saw Baily lying in the deep shade of a wild cherry
tree. His face was turned away from me. I thought he was
sleeping.

But Spider, still stretched out on the table in the cook
shack, faced me. He wasn't limp and relaxed like Baily.
Instead, he seemed brittle and tense. Suddenly I was certain he had not slept at all, but had been watching me the
whole time.

A sudden wind trembled in the willow, and a cloud
shadow passed across the great basin that held the lake
and the cabin and us three runaways. I shuddered.

ℱIVE

ℬaily built a fire in the cook shack, and I heated canned spaghetti and meatballs for our dinner. While my grandparents had been alive, we hadn't relied only on the canned food stored in the cabin. Every day we had driven to town for meat, fresh vegetables and fruit, and wonderful bread from the little bakery a block away from the bus depot. After Grandpa died, Grandma arranged with the caretaker, Justine, to drive us to town every other day for fresh food and a good visit with our friends in the shops.

But those days were past, and sometimes I wondered if my former life hadn't been a dream in which everything was peaceful and predictable. The tall quiet house in San Francisco, my school and the friends I'd made there, the annual visits to the lake—all parts of a serene dream.

Reality was Gerald and Hope and their two spoiled sons. Reality was Gerald bursting into my bedroom whenever he felt like it.

Reality was Gerald driving away with the chain saw in his truck and coming back to shout, "Look what you made me do, Jocelyn!" And I had known before I went to look that the tree with the heron's nest had been cut down.

"Are you okay?" Baily asked.

I flinched. I had been stirring the spaghetti mindlessly until it was nearly mush.

"It'll be ready in a minute," I said. I shielded my face from the heat that shimmered out of the stove and concentrated on what I was doing. "Will somebody set the table?" I asked.

"Sure." That was Baily. Spider had offered no help of any sort, but instead had jittered and paced, complaining about canned food, bugs, the afternoon heat, and his suspicion that something was crawling through the brush at the edge of the woods, watching us.

"It could be a cougar," he said, warming to the subject again. "It could be a bear. I never heard anything like that when I was here before."

"It's probably your mother, looking for you with a hatchet," Baily offered with a small, cold smile. He had carried dinner plates from the cabin without my asking him, and now set three places at the table.

I pointed my wooden spoon at Spider. "Did you bring jeans with you?" I cried. "Go put them on right this minute. You've got mosquito bites all over your legs, and I'll bet that's why you're whining all the time. And use some of the bug spray in the cabin. You'll cheer up if you quit itching. At least maybe you'll shut up."

Spider galloped away, with his arms, shirt, and hair flapping. I sighed while I watched him snatch his backpack from the porch and carry it into the cabin.

"I can run him off, if you want," Baily said. "But he's so weird, he'll probably do something to get even."

"Tell the sheriff about me?" I asked. "I wouldn't put it past him. But then, maybe you're thinking about phoning your parents and telling them everything."

I hoped Baily would protest, but he didn't. He bent to brush dust off the benches and finally sat down, facing away from me, looking toward the woods.

"Do you think Spider's right and something's out there?" I asked. Gerald? Could he have remembered the place?

"No. I think Spider is like a radio that's always tuned between stations, making a racket that drives everybody nuts."

"Maybe," I said. I glanced at Baily and saw by his expression that his doubts about Spider were as serious as mine. There was something about the kid, something strange that I couldn't understand. I was certain he was older than he admitted. But why should he lie?

Spider loped back, wearing jeans and a long-sleeved gray shirt that hung almost to his knees.

"I can't stand mosquitoes," he said, slapping at his neck. "You don't know where they've been, right? It's not as if you could ask them who they bit just before they bit you. I mean, they could have had their last meal off somebody who had AIDS. Did you ever think of that?"

"No," Baily grumbled, "because it's stupid. And I'm not going to start worrying now about where mosquitos have been before they bite me. Did you use that bug spray?"

"No way," Spider declared. "It's full of chemicals that cause cancer. It says right on the can not to get it in your eyes or mouth. Why do you think it says that? Because it's poisonous, that's why. If it doesn't give you cancer, then it makes you go blind. You hear about things like that happening to people. Boy, not me. I'm careful about what I put on me."

Baily stared at him, hard. "You've been griping ever since you got here. Now you're worried about getting AIDS or cancer or going blind. What next? Do you ever have a good time?"

Spider spread his hands in a helpless gesture. "Complaining about stuff is what I do best, okay?"

"No," Baily said. "It's not okay. Knock it off."

Spider ignored him and danced around the table. "Are we having dessert? What's dinner if we don't have dessert? Have you got cookies or Ding Dongs, something like that?"

"I've got *applesauce*," I said. "If you're so worried about poisons, why do you eat store-bought pastry? Or potato chips, for heaven's sake? You don't make any sense." I handed him the can and can opener. "Pour it out in that blue bowl on the table."

He obeyed, humming tunelessly while he fiddled with the can opener. Baily and I exchanged a long, exasperated look.

"What are we doing tonight for excitement?" Spider asked as he sat down and tucked his paper napkin under his chin. He grinned, showing beautiful straight teeth. For the first time, I noticed that his ears were pierced.

He's ridiculous, I thought as I served myself. He must drive his mother crazy. Maybe she threw him out so she could hear herself think for once.

Spider talked with his mouth full, babbling throughout dinner about better meals he'd had, always due to his own hard work, of course, and nearly always made up of strange combinations of junk food.

"You sound like an environmentalist having a nightmare," I told him.

Spider laughed, but Baily was watching dozens of small bats swooping over the lake after insects and hadn't heard me—or so I believed.

The sun disappeared in the midst of a smoldering heap of clouds. A shadowless twilight followed swiftly, and the loon called out several times, piercing the gray silence. I brought out the candles and Grandma's silver candelabra without explanation. The boys watched while I set the white candles on the railing around the cabin and then lit them, one by one.

"This is the way my grandmother did it," I said. "So it's the way I do it now."

"Why…" Spider began.

"Shut up," Baily said.

They watched while I lit the candelabra. The flames burned steadily and faintly scented the air with bayberry.

"Now I'm going out in the boat," I said. "The way we always did. You can come along, but you can't talk."

Spider sat in the bow, his skinny legs folded close together, and gnawed on a hangnail. Baily took his place in the stern, so sure-footed he barely rocked the boat. I

bent over the oars and rowed smoothly, almost silently.
Halfway to the island, I stopped and we drifted.

The cabin, surrounded by candles, seemed to float in
the middle of a dark ocean, a strange, square derelict abandoned by phantom sailors. The flames, reflected in the
lake, might actually have been burning deep in some
underwater fairy kingdom.

The lopsided moon overhead shone in the water like
a lantern sunk deep below the boat. Stars glimmered above
and flickered in the lake. Sky and water had no boundaries.
In the silence, time slowed. The wheel of stars shifted.

"Jocelyn, what was the best time you ever had?"
Spider asked softly.

It was such a strange question that I didn't answer at
first. Finally I said, "I'll tell my best time if both of you tell
yours, too."

"Okay," Spider said. "But I go last."

"Jocelyn goes first," Baily said.

"It was here at the lake," I said, "when my grandfather was still alive. He was a singer..."

"What kind of singer?" Spider asked.

Baily groaned. "Let *her* talk."

"He was an opera tenor," I said. "The man who
owned the hotel on the lake east of here was a friend of his,
and every year Grandpa would sing once for the hotel
guests. They were mostly old people who'd been going
there for years and years, and they remembered Grandpa
from when he still performed on the stage all over the
world. Anyway, he sang once a year for them, but not at
the hotel. They'd come here in boats, and they'd carry can-

dles. You could see them coming, this long line of lights bobbing on the water. Then they'd drift around out here, and Grandpa would stand on the porch and play his guitar and sing for them."

"And there'd be candles on the porch, too," Spider said with obvious satisfaction, as if he'd seen it all himself.

"Yes," I said. "White candles all around. Gran-auntie and I went out in a boat once so we could see and hear what the others saw and heard. Grandpa didn't sing opera arias here. He sang romantic songs from old-fashioned musicals. That's what everybody wanted to hear. The time I remember best—the time I was happiest—he sang a song about sunrise, even though it was dark. 'Softly, as in a morning sunrise.' I remember those words. Gran-auntie started to cry. It was very beautiful."

And, I thought, I believed everything would stay that way forever. Gerald was only a name.

A star fell, surprising me. "Look there!" I said. "See it?"

But the boys missed it. The boat drifted between sky and water, gently, tangled in the night.

"Once my brother took me fishing with him," Baily said suddenly, out of the darkness and silence. "It was early one morning. We went to his favorite place, where the river runs under a rusty old railroad trestle. It was misty, and colder than I thought it would be. My brother cast his line without a hook. I didn't know he fished without a hook until then. I asked him why, but he said I'd figure it out for myself. The best part was standing there with him, not talking, watching the line, listening to the water. Everything was the way it's supposed to be."

"Safe," I whispered. Baily didn't respond. Perhaps he had not heard me.

"Why didn't he use a hook?" Spider asked. "Did you figure it out?"

"I was telling about the best time I ever had," Baily said. "A hook wasn't part of it."

"Why..." Spider began again.

"It's your turn to tell," I interrupted.

Spider cleared his throat but didn't say anything.

"Your turn, Spider," I prompted.

"The best time I ever had was when I found an envelope with a hundred bucks in it in the gutter outside the main post office in Seattle," Spider said. "I kept it."

"You're a real winner," Baily growled in disgust.

Spider is lying, I thought. He doesn't want us to know about his best time. I felt outraged, as if he had robbed me of something precious and refused to share his own wealth with me, offering me a bit of trash instead. Maybe he was even laughing at me. At Baily, too.

Had he ever told us the truth about anything?

"Time to go back," I said abruptly. "It's getting cold."

Baily chose to spend the night in the cook shack, where he had slept the night before.

"But Spider sleeps somewhere else," he said. "I don't care where, just as long as it's not with me or anywhere near me."

"Hey," Spider said. "I got no problem with that. The cook shack doesn't have a roof, only that arbor thing. If it rains, I plan on staying dry. I'll sleep in the storage shed. I saw an old lawn swing in there."

I blew out all the candles and carried them inside the cabin, then shut the door without saying good night to the boys. I was close to crying, sorry I had told them about Grandpa and the people in the boats. All that belonged to another life, the perfect one that seemed so unreal now. Had I ever been that safe? Had life ever made so much sense?

I crawled into bed and hugged my pillow to my chest. Tomorrow was Sunday. All I had to do was make it through that day and half of the next. I'd call Gran-auntie exactly at two o'clock, just as we had agreed. By then Gran-auntie would be my legal guardian until Dad got back at Christmas, and I would be going home to San Francisco. I wouldn't even stop by Hope's for my clothes— I wouldn't risk it. The nightmare would be over.

I slept hard, without dreaming, and woke at dawn, shivering in the cold. For a moment I didn't recognize my surroundings. Was I in the cabin?

"Gran?" I called out softly. The window seat Grandma always used for a bed wasn't even made up.

And then I remembered everything.

I got up stiffly and pulled open the cabin door. Wood smoke drifted lazily across the slope from the cook shack. Baily was up before me. His sleeping bag lay tumbled on the porch close to the door.

He had heated a small pan of water and made a mug of instant coffee for himself, but when he saw me coming, he offered it to me. I wrapped my hands around it grate-fully.

"Oh, that's so good," I said after tasting it. "My sister

won't let me drink it, but my grandmother always did."

"You think about the past a lot, don't you?" Baily asked.

I should have been offended, but I wasn't. Thinking about the past saved me, kept me going. If I hadn't had a past worth remembering, I couldn't have endured the two years in my sister's house.

Fortunately, Baily didn't seem to want an answer. Silent and preoccupied, he made another cup of coffee for himself.

"You slept on the porch, didn't you?" I asked.

"I didn't bother you," he said defensively.

"You were supposed to stay in the cook shack," I said.

"That kid," he said. He shook his head. "I didn't trust him. And now he's gone."

"Spider?" I looked at Baily over the rim of the mug. "Gone?"

This is trouble, I thought. Why didn't I leave the minute Spider showed up here? "Did he take his stuff with him?" I asked.

"Yeah, I think so," Baily said. "I bet he left last night."

I got to my feet, still feeling stiff, although the sun was up now. "There's no telling what Spider will do, so I've got to leave."

"Where will you go?"

I didn't know yet, but I wasn't going to admit it. "I've got something in mind," I said. "You can go on back to Seattle."

I hurried toward the cabin, running the possibilities

through my mind. I could stay in the woods. It would only be for one more night. Or I could go back to Seattle, call Gran-auntie from there, and ask her to make arrangements so I could stay in the hotel. I should have done that to begin with.

No. Gerald or the police would find me for sure if I stayed in a hotel. A teenager alone would be too obvious.

I folded my bedding swiftly and shoved it in the window seat. My swimsuit was still hanging on the porch railing. I put it and the other articles of clothing I had scattered around in my bag. I'd have to get the dishes and pans from the cook shack, and put them and the candles away. And don't forget to do something about the trash, I reminded myself. But what? I couldn't take it with me, not if I wasn't going into town.

Suddenly I stopped and shook my head angrily. I was worrying about trash at a time like this?

The boat. I'd better not leave it to Baily to put away. I ran back to the cook shack, intending to gather up the dishes and pans, but Baily was carrying them toward me.

"I'm going with you," he said.

"No," I said.

"You could come home with me," he said.

"No way," I said. I wasn't so stupid I'd trap myself. "I'm leaving now, by myself. But I need you to help me with the boat."

"Hey, look what I got!"

Spider. He was back, galloping in his clumsy way, carrying a grocery bag in both arms. "I got breakfast, lunch, and dinner!" he shouted. "Real food, not canned stuff. And potato chips, lots of potato chips!"

If he noticed our amazement, he ignored it. He emptied the bag on the table and said, "Ta-da! Danish and orange juice and wieners and hot dog buns and mustard and..."

"We thought you'd run out on us," I said. I wondered if he could hear my heart hammering.

Spider, busy pawing through his supplies, grinned without looking up. "You thought I turned you in for the reward," he said.

"What reward?" I asked, sick with fright.

Spider laughed. "No reward, girl," he said. "At least, not that I heard of. No 'Wanted' posters, either. Half the town's asleep and the other half's getting ready for church. Come on, let's eat. I admit that I already had breakfast at a fast-food place, but it wasn't that good, and I'm hungry again."

"You couldn't be worried about being caught if you wandered all over town," Baily said.

"I was safe enough."

"Where did you spend the night?" I asked. I helped myself to a Danish and a carton of juice.

"Right where I told you I would!" Spider cried, outraged.

"Your stuff's gone," Baily said.

"It's folded up and put away, all neat and tidy," Spider said. "Go look inside the shed beside the lawn swing. Go look if you don't believe me! I didn't leave a mess!"

I believed him because he was so angry. He seemed

to think we were more concerned about his being messy than running off. So he had slept where he'd said he would. Fine.

But he had gone clear to town for odds and ends of groceries. I couldn't imagine walking two miles each way for pastry, fresh juice, and hot dogs.

"I don't believe you went into town just for food," I said harshly. "You're up to something and I want to know what it is, right now."

Spider swallowed the mouthful of Danish he'd just bitten off. "I'm not up to anything," he cried. "I got up early so I could do something nice for you and Baily. Why don't you say 'thanks' instead of accusing me of something? But no, no, you don't do that. No! Instead, you think I ran off so I could tell Mr. Policeman that yes, they're out there all right, Jocelyn and Baily, keeping house in this old falling-down cabin with no running water and no plumbing and no electricity. You really think somebody cares you're out here? *Nobody* cares. You're not as important as you like to think you are, you Jocelyn, with your grandma and your grandpa and all your lousy white candles!"

I could not have been more shocked if he had slapped me. I was speechless, and could only stare at him.

Spider's eyes glinted with angry tears. "You make me sick, you do, you spoiled brat!"

Baily brought his fist down on the table, hard. "Shut up," he told Spider. "You're the only spoiled brat here, and if you don't shut up, I'll throw you in the shed and lock the door on you. You won't be running into town then, and we won't have to listen to you anymore. Do you understand me? Now tell Jocelyn you're sorry you shot off your big mouth about her and her family."

A tear streaked to Spider's chin. "Okay," he said. "Okay, I'm sorry."

He picked up his plate and stalked away then. But I heard him whisper furiously, *"You Jocelyn!"* as if my name were a curse.

$\mathcal{S}$ IX

No one wanted lunch because all three of us had eaten so much breakfast. At noon, I told the boys I was going to swim to the other side of the lake, and they could do as they pleased. There were swimsuits in the cabin they could use.

"I'll come with you," Baily said.

"Not me," Spider announced. He twitched his shoulders and attacked his hangnail again. "I hate swimming. Who knows what might be in the water underneath you? Something could reach up and rip off your legs. What if there's a Loch Ness monster in this lake? Nobody'd even find your bones. Don't you ever think about that when you're way out in the water and nobody's close enough to grab you if you need help?"

I shook my head. "No, I don't think about things like that, and I can't figure out why you do. You seem to spend all your time looking for the bogeyman, and I wish you'd quit talking about it."

I left him behind and went to the cabin to find a

swimsuit for Baily. Baily followed me as far as the door and waited on the porch, silent and grave. If he was worried about the Loch Ness monster, he kept it to himself.

I found half a dozen swimsuits that would fit him in the cupboard under the window seat. I picked a blue one and tossed it to him, then shut the door. Let him change somewhere else. Through the window, I saw him jogging toward the storage shed.

Spider wandered, knock-kneed, along the shore, exhibiting a great interest in what he saw there among the reeds and wild irises. Pollen and small insects rose around him, glimmering like gold dust in the sunlight.

Maybe, I thought, Spider's searching for evidence of the monster. Human bones picked clean? Scraps of clothing and shoes with teeth marks? I grinned.

Then I saw the heron. This time I was certain it wasn't my imagination. It stood deep in the reeds, one leg bent, concentrating on something in the water.

And then I saw that Spider was standing on the other side of the reeds, resting his weight on one leg, also concentrating on the water. He and the bird, mirroring one another, were unaware of each other.

The sight delighted me, and I was sorry Baily wasn't nearby so I could point it out. I watched until the heron finally saw Spider and rose into the air, shrieking raucously. Spider panicked and ran, his skinny arms, hands, feet, and shirt all flapping. I laughed aloud.

When I came out in my swimsuit, Baily was waiting, sitting on a rock and tossing pebbles into the water. Spider was nearly out of sight, floundering through wildflowers on his way toward the upper end of the lake.

"You sure you don't want to take the boat at least as far as the island?" Baily asked. "You—we might get tired coming back."

He was right. I'd never swum so far, and I couldn't imagine what possessed me to make it sound as if I could.

I can't let either of them get the idea I'm weak or afraid, I thought. They have to believe I'm a match for anything. No, I have to believe it. "If you need to use the boat, it's all right with me," I said.

I rowed again, and Baily made no argument about it. He sat on the cushions in the bottom of the boat and leaned back, watching the sky.

I avoided looking at him. I couldn't let him learn that the longer I was at the cabin, the more uncertain I felt. I didn't know what was happening in Seattle. Hope couldn't have gone on the church retreat, not without me at home watching the boys. She'd be angry that her free baby-sitter had spoiled her plans.

Gerald would be wondering how much I had told about him. And to whom I had told it. He'd be inventing ways of twisting the truth to suit his own purposes. "The best defense is a good offense," he had told me once after he had won an argument with a neighbor in front of fifty people at a barbecue.

Even though it was still the weekend, Gran-auntie might have found Dad by now. She would have started calling before Hope did, so she could have found him first. Gran-auntie would tell him the truth. Well, part of the truth. She'd tell him what she knew, that I was sick of

Gerald yelling at me, and praying over me, and making me do all the work, and not letting me have friends or go anywhere, and blaming me for everything. All that yelling. There was never an end to the yelling.

But I could have borne it. Only Gerald went too far.

"What are you thinking about?" Baily asked.

"About final straws," I said.

He got up and sat in the stern, facing me. He was so tan, he looked as if he spent all his time outside. Light reflected off the lake into his face, and his eyes gleamed like deep, clear water. I saw a scar on his chin, near his mouth, before I looked away.

"That's why you're here," he said. "Because of a final straw. Because of the heron?"

I squinted up at the burning sky and then looked back over my shoulder. The island was close. I pulled the oars in and let the boat bump into land gently.

"Come on," I said, scrambling over the bow and pulling the rope with me.

He followed, padding behind me under the willow and across the island. The ducks scattered noisily and took off, flapping away. I plunged into the water and began the steady, strong crawl my grandfather had taught me years before.

Baily wasted energy with too much splashing, and I pulled away from him easily. Good, I thought. I'm in charge. This is my place, and I'm the best swimmer, and I'm not afraid of anything. There's nothing I can't handle.

There was a three-foot bank to climb on the other shore, but I scrambled up easily. Baily was close behind when I stood at the edge of the meadow that stretched south to the foothills. The tall grass was embroidered with every color of wildflower I could imagine.

"I never saw so many flowers," Baily said, shading his eyes.

I waded out into the meadow, where the flowers came to my hips. "See the rocks ahead?" I asked. "That's where we always sat."

I led him to three smooth boulders that stuck up out of the grass and flowers. "We called these the Family. See this one, the biggest? You can sit on it as if it were a chair. This is Papa. And this one, the Mama, you can lean against. The Baby makes a good footstool."

Baily ran his hand over the Papa rock. "It's so smooth," he said. "It feels polished."

"Grandpa said the glacier did that, sliding over the rocks. There's a rock with a hole scooped in it beside the middle lake, and a tree grows through it."

Baily sprawled in the rock chair and looked into the distance. "Nobody lives at the middle lake, right?"

"No one ever did. The man who owned the upper lake, the one that had the hotel beside it, owned the middle lake, too. Or at least he did years ago. Maybe he's dead by now."

"And he burned down his hotel."

"Well, that's what people said. The hotel was gone the last time we were here, and no one can ever build anything new on the three lakes. It's got something to do with the environmental laws. The cabin belongs to me now, and it can be repaired, but it can't ever be replaced. At least, that's what Gran-auntie told me." I leaned back on Mama rock and closed my eyes. "Everything here will go back to nature. I think that's nice."

"Nobody came out to your cabin last year," Baily said. "Is that right?"

My eyes snapped open. What had possessed me to talk so much? "No, no one came last year," I said. "Gran-auntie couldn't find a caretaker after Justine moved away. Why do you want to know?"

He shook his head slowly, not looking at me. "Just thinking things over," he said.

"Well, don't," I said. "Don't think about me."

"Easy to say," he muttered.

I sat up straight. "What does that mean?" I asked.

"Nothing."

I knew from his expression that he wouldn't say more. He didn't talk enough and Spider talked too much. And so did I.

I had left my watch in the cabin, and I tried to guess the time. We had left about noon. Surely it wasn't one o'clock yet. Okay, that meant that I had twenty-five hours to go before I'd be talking to Gran-auntie. The first thing I'd ask is, "Are you my guardian now?" The next question would be, "What time does my flight leave?"

How had things turned into such a mess? Had it been my fault from the beginning? Gerald and Hope always said it was.

Hope was my sister! My sister! Well, half-sister. But that didn't matter. Why hadn't she helped me?

I fidgeted restlessly. The sun here was really too hot. I'd be sunburned if we didn't start back soon.

Okay, so why hadn't Hope believed me? I hadn't just hinted around. I'd told her right out what Gerald was doing. But Hope had let me fight him alone. How could she do that?

Well, I was more than capable of defending myself. The one thing Gerald couldn't stand was hearing anybody yell as loudly as he did. Especially if it was about something he didn't want all the neighbors hearing. Jerk. He was a jerk.

I sat up. "Let's go back. It's too hot to stay here."

"Look," Baily said, pointing to the southwest. A long line of black clouds seethed on the horizon. "There's going to be a thunderstorm."

I grinned. "Good. You should see the lake then. It's terrific."

Baily grinned, too. "But let's not be out in it when the storm hits, okay?"

We ran back through the meadow together and once, when I stumbled, Baily grabbed my hand. And held it a little too long. I yanked my hand free and pushed ahead of him to be first in the water.

When we reached the cabin, I found a clean shirt and socks for Baily and insisted he take them. "You can't wear the same clothes all the time," I said. "I wish I had jeans that would fit you, but you're too tall."

His face turned red under his tan. "I'll return the clothes after I've washed them," he said.

"I won't be here after tomorrow, remember? Anyway, all the clothes here are old. Grandma never cared if people visiting us didn't bring them back."

"You can't get on with your life, can you?" he asked. "You can't get over what you once had." He was facing out over the lake, holding the shirt and socks casually, as if he didn't care about anything, including my answer. But I knew he did.

"You ask too many questions," I said. "Maybe I like remembering how things were more than you do because I have better things to remember."

Baily shrugged and walked off, heading for the storage shed. If I had hoped to offend him—and I wasn't certain if that had been my intention—I had failed.

I shut the cabin door and changed out of my swimsuit into faded old shorts and a ragged cotton shirt I found in the window seat. I hung my swimsuit over the porch railing and sat down at the table. Half the sky was black now, and a strong wind disturbed the lake. A few yellow willow leaves blew out over the water.

Where was Spider? I couldn't see him anywhere, and I'd have heard him talking if he'd been in the storage shed when Baily went in to change. He'd be sorry if he got caught in the thunderstorm.

Baily came back, swinging his wet swimsuit. He tossed it over the railing next to mine and sat opposite me at the table.

"Did you see Spider?" I asked.

He shook his head, opened his mouth as if to say something, then closed it again.

"Go ahead, say whatever's on your mind," I said.

"He's got a padlock on his backpack."

I stared at him. "You wanted to go through his things?"

"You bet," Baily said. "He went through the pockets in my jeans."

"You're kidding," I said. "How could you tell?"

"I keep my house key in my back left pocket. I found it in the right pocket."

"Did he take anything?"

Baily shook his head. "Nope. All my money's still in my wallet. I don't think he's a thief. But there's something going on with him."

I hurried inside to check on my own things. I'd hidden my wallet, along with my calling card, under the loose floorboard in the far corner. They were still there, apparently untouched.

I heard the first roll of thunder when I returned to the porch. Rain fell immediately, pouring off the roof in silvery sheets. The lake erupted into rough, slashing waves that pounded against the shore. The island disappeared into the storm.

"Isn't this great?" I asked. I leaned against the railing, and when it creaked under my weight, I retreated and sat at the table. Thunder followed lightning by only a second. Across the lake, the sky was forked open by jagged light.

"There used to be a dogwood tree on the island," I said. "Grandpa planted it, too, just like the willow. But lightning struck it. Gran-auntie cried, because dogwoods are her favorite trees."

"You could plant another one out there," Baily said.

"They have to be planted in spring," I said. "Grandpa came up from San Francisco in April to put the dogwood in, and he didn't tell anybody until we got here in August. He loved surprising us."

Lightning flickered wildly and the thunder that followed grumbled on and on. The porch rocked a little.

"Someday the pilings have to be replaced," I said.

Baily laughed shortly. "It better be soon. I don't think this place can last through many more summer storms, and the winter ones are a lot worse."

Will I ever come here again? I wondered. It seemed to me, in that moment, that I never would. This will be the last of it, I thought, and not because the pilings are in such bad condition. Something else is reaching an end. I shouldn't have come this time. I should have left my memories perfect the way they were, and not mixed them up with trouble.

Oh please, don't let anything bad happen.

Where had that thought come from? I shivered from cold and got up, to blunder inside and grab my denim jacket.

"Are you cold?" I called out. "Do you want a sweater?"

"Jeez," Baily snarled. "Look who's coming."

I hurried out. He pointed to the east, where Spider, sopping and bedraggled, stumbled toward them over the rocky shore.

He looks like a puppet with broken strings, I thought, close to laughter.

Lightning flared and thunder rocked the world. Spider uttered a thin, high cry and flung himself forward.

"I nearly got killed!" he cried as he scrambled to the porch. "Lightning hit a tree six inches away from me, or maybe even closer."

"Serves you right," Baily observed. He leaned back, watching the water, pointedly ignoring Spider's distress.

I thought of offering the boy dry clothes, but he had his own in the shed. Let him take care of himself, I thought, glancing covertly at him, wondering if he could.

Spider hugged himself, shaking with cold. His wet T-shirt clung to his back, and I could see that he wore something underneath, a vest perhaps. I nearly asked what it was but then changed my mind. He'd answer with a dozen questions of his own.

The rain stopped as abruptly as it had begun. The lightning was farther away now, and the thunder lagged behind it several seconds. In the south, the dark clouds tore apart, showing bright blue behind them. Sunlight poured through the gap and flickered on the rough lake. On the island, a bird sang.

"Show's over," Baily said softly.

Spider sneezed dramatically. "Now I'm coming down with a cold. I hate catching colds, because I always get earaches and then I have to use nose drops and take pills. This is the worst vacation I ever had in my entire life."

"Go change into dry clothes!" I cried. "You are the most helpless baby I ever saw. I never knew such a pain in the neck."

"I brought you the hot dogs for our dinner!" Spider yelled back. "You wouldn't be looking forward to a good dinner if it wasn't for me."

"While you were gone, some raccoon probably wandered into the cook shack and ate them," I said.

Spider gawked at me for a moment, then took off running.

Sighing, I watched him gallop off. "When he runs, he looks as if bits and pieces of him were going to start falling off."

Baily laughed abruptly, then stopped. "Hot dogs," he said, shaking his head. "What a fuss."

"Don't you like them?"

"Sure," he said. "The only reason *I* hope a raccoon got them is because Spider will go crazy over it."

"They're still here!" Spider shrieked from the cook shack. He waved something in the air. "They're still here!"

"I bet they can hear him clear to Seattle," I said.

Baily laughed and shook his head. "He must drive his parents and teachers up the wall," he said.

We sat in silence for a while, and then Baily said, "You went to boarding school in San Francisco?"

"I was a day student," I said. "I loved being there." I glanced at my watch. In less than twenty-four hours, I'd be on my way back where I belonged.

"If you'd told people how Gerald was treating you, you could have been back at that school sooner."

I stared at him. "Are you starting up with that again?"

He shook his head wordlessly and looked away. Maybe he had guessed the truth. He might have decided that what had been happening to me was partly my fault. People thought that. And even if they didn't, they still had problems with the whole subject. It seemed strange to me that when a girl complained about being hit on by a man, the person she complained to ended up feeling as embarrassed as the girl did. Embarrassed instead of angry. Or maybe the person felt embarrassed first and then angry later.

But that wasn't how people reacted if a girl complained when someone had struck her or stolen her money. Then they were angry immediately.

"I could handle Gerald," I told Baily bitterly. "What I couldn't handle was that my sister acted as if she didn't believe me. Or maybe she did, but it was too much trouble taking my side."

"What about your dad?" Baily was still looking away, probably because he couldn't stand the sight of somebody whose brother-in-law was as crazy as mine. Gerald definitely was not a social asset.

"You know my dad works in Germany—but now he's in Italy for a while. I told him I hated Gerald—that he treats me like a maid and won't let me have friends. But what's he supposed to do when he's so far away? And, of course, good old Gerald would only say I'm lying. And Hope will take Gerald's side. She always does."

"Don't you have anybody to help you?"

"Gran-auntie, in San Francisco. She's helping me." But she's so old, I thought. I couldn't imagine that she'd ever heard of anything as bad as what Gerald was trying to do.

I didn't tell her about the heron's nest, either, because

I didn't think I could without crying. Maybe she wouldn't understand how bad I felt, because it had been my fault. The herons didn't know anything about human beings and the mean things we do. They thought they were safe, they and their baby.

He was big enough to fly. He could have survived. Of course he did! I only thought I saw feathers. My eyes filled with tears suddenly.

"So what was the final straw?" Baily asked. He was looking directly at me. "You didn't answer me before. Was it really the heron?"

How could he even ask? I wiped my tears away with the backs of my hands and stared at him as insolently as I could manage. "Okay. My sister was going away for ten days and I was supposed to take care of her bratty little boys and do all the cooking and put up with Gerald's yelling. I couldn't see my friends. I couldn't go anywhere. So I decided to cut out."

I'd gone to see the place where the nest had been. The tree lay flat, and the nest had been demolished, nothing more than a scattering of sticks tangled with branches and underbrush. The woods were so silent! Behind me, acres of flat bare mud decorated with surveyors' stakes stretched to the highway. Ahead of me lay more land, thick with trees—and silence—as far as the creek. A quarter of a mile away, out of sight, Gerald's house sat in the middle of a lawn as perfect as a carpet. He had won.

No one would ever be able to understand how I had felt at that moment. Gerald had been right. This was my fault. I shouldn't have argued with him. He knew the most effective way of punishing me was hurting something I loved. I should have anticipated what he'd do. I had a right to defend myself from him, but I should have led him toward a different sacrifice.

But what did I have left? He had already denied me friends, hobbies, books, television, and music. Bit by bit he had tightened the noose around me. His behavior was unacceptable, but when I refused to accept it, he punished me. No matter which way I turned, I was trapped.

Why didn't Hope help me?

After I saw what Gerald had done, I went straight from the woods to the nearest convenience store and called Gran-auntie to tell her I was running away and wanted to return to San Francisco.

What other choice did I have?

Baily was standing too close. I could see the gold flecks in his eyes. "What are you going to tell people when they ask you what really happened?" he asked.

"Shut up," I said, choking on the words. There was no way in the world anyone could understand about Gerald, and then there was the heron. I had been responsible for its death. I had goaded Gerald and he had done what I should have known he'd do. I might just as well have taken his gun and shot the bird.

"Hey, you two!" Spider cried. "It's time for dinner! Let's start a fire. I want hot dogs!"

$\mathcal{S}$EVEN

"$\mathcal{I}$t's too early for dinner," I said. The sun was still high and I was too hot to be interested in food.

"How about you?" Spider asked Baily. "Don't you want to eat?" He jittered while he talked, fiddled with his hat, tore at his hangnail.

Baily stared him down. "I don't care when I eat."

"I'll start the fire," Spider said. "I'll even set the table. But let's eat before I pass out from hunger. I can't go this long without food."

"Would you stop talking if you were unconscious?" I asked. "Should we make some plans about you lying flat on your back with your eyes closed?"

Spider's laugh was high and nervous. "Come on, come on. Let's eat."

"It's not worth arguing about." I headed for the cook shack, with Spider dancing along behind me, humming and pawing at his hat.

Baily pushed the boy aside when Spider repeated that he'd start the fire to cook the hot dogs. "Sit down before somebody knocks you down," Baily said. "And don't talk."

I brought an old iron frying pan from the cabin and would have put the wieners in it, but Spider raised a howl. "No, no, we got to cook them on sticks! They don't count as real hot dogs unless we cook them on sticks."

"We don't have sticks," I said.

"I'll cut them, I'll cut them!" Spider yelled. "Baily, you give me your knife and I'll bring us back some good sticks. I know right where to get them."

"In your dreams," Baily grumbled. He'd been stacking kindling in the stove, but he stopped, sighed, and loped off toward the woods.

"Then I'll start the fire," Spider said as he grabbed a piece of kindling and poked it into the tentlike arrangement Baily had made. He yelled in surprise when the neat pile collapsed.

"Sit down!" I shouted. "Sit and don't do anything, because you're driving us crazy. How old are you, anyway? You act like a two-year-old."

Spider sulked while I set the table. When Baily returned with several strong alder sticks already sharpened to points, Spider elaborately ignored him, fingering his pierced earlobes while he watched swallows darting over the lake.

Baily said nothing when he saw what was left of his fire preparations. He built the pile of kindling again, and lit one of the wooden matches I handed him. The fire smoked and crackled, then died out. Baily tried again, and then once more before the fire finally caught. He added several small logs and the flames leaped up eagerly.

"Can we start now?" Spider asked. "It's taken Baily three hours to do what I could have done in three minutes. I want to eat! I'm hungry."

"You have to wait until there are hot coals," I told him. "Haven't you ever done this before?"

"Only a million times, that's all," Spider said. "Maybe two million." He was on his feet again, sorting through the sticks Baily had brought back. "Here's a good one. I'll…" He stumbled over his own feet and lurched against Baily.

Everything happened so fast that I barely understood what went wrong. Baily began falling backward, flinging out his arms for balance. He caught himself, but not before the flames touched one of his hands. He cried out and leaped away from the hearth.

"You're burned!" I cried.

Baily cradled his left hand against his chest and bit his lower lip savagely.

"Darn you, Spider!" I shouted, reaching to slap the boy, but missing when he ducked.

"I'm sorry, I'm sorry!" Spider shrieked. "It wasn't my fault!"

"Let me see your hand," I told Baily. "I've got first-aid supplies in the cabin, but we need cold water first. Here, let me pump some over your hand. The well water's cold as ice."

"Yes, yes, put water on it," Spider babbled. "Lots of water. Water's good."

Baily held his hand under the water while I worked the pump handle furiously. Blisters rose on his fingers while I watched in horror.

"You need a doctor," I said. "We'll start for town right now."

"Let's go, let's go," Spider cried. "Come on, Baily. We'll get you fixed up quick."

"No," Baily said. He examined his fingers and winced at the sight. "Can you pump more water, Jocelyn? It felt so good."

"I'll pump as long as you want me to, but I think we should try to get you to a doctor."

"We'll never find a doctor on a Sunday," Baily said.

"Then we'll go to the hospital emergency room," I said.

"The hospital closed last year," Spider said. "We'll have to find a doctor."

I stared at Spider. "How do you know the hospital closed?"

Spider froze, panicked. Then he licked his lips, grinned lopsidedly, and said, "Hey, I told you I been here lots of times. I know everything about the towns around here. Where all the fast-food joints are, all that good stuff."

"Oh, shut up," I said. "Nobody's interested in food now. Is there a doctor nearby?"

Spider shrugged and held his hands up helplessly. "I guess so. I don't know for sure because I never needed one."

"Well, you're going to need one in a minute," I cried. "All this was your fault. Now get out of here and stay away. We don't want you hanging around. All you do is make trouble."

I raised my hand again as if I would slap him, and Spider ducked and ran off, squealing.

"You're pretty tough," Baily said, laughing a little.

"Not tough enough where Spider's concerned," I said.
I worked the pump, watching water gush over Baily's
burn. "How do your fingers feel? Is this helping?"

"It feels good," Baily said. "Just don't stop."

The sight of the blisters sickened me. "I should have
made that creep Spider pump water while I went in to get
the first-aid kit," I said. "Maybe there's something in there
that would help more."

"I'll be fine," Baily said. "Don't worry. This isn't the
worst thing that ever happened to me."

Hoping to distract him from his blisters, I said, "Tell
me about the worst thing."

With his free hand, he touched the scar on his chin.
"I got this sledding when I was a kid. Lots of blood but
that's all."

I looked up at him. His gaze met mine, and I stopped
pumping water. For a moment I didn't breathe.

"Are you going to be all right?" I asked. My voice
shook.

"Maybe not," he whispered. "Maybe I'll never be all
right."

"I'm sorry!" I cried, and I raised the pump handle
again.

"Stop," he said. I stopped.

"It's not because of my hand," he said soberly.

"What then?" Did he mean he wouldn't be all right
because of this weekend? Because of me? Water dripped
slowly into the stone basin and drained away.

He shook his head as if suddenly waking up.

"Nothing," he said. "Never mind." He examined his fingers and bent them experimentally. "I'll be okay, but maybe I ought to put bandages over the blisters. If you've got them."

"Wait here." I ran to the cabin, passing Spider on the porch. He was wiggling a railing back and forth, behaving exactly the way my sister's boys would, fiddling with something already half broken until they finally succeeded in destroying it.

"Leave that alone," I told Spider.

"*What!*" he yelled. "I'm not doing anything! Why are you always nagging me?"

I didn't bother answering. Even if Spider understood what a pest he was, I doubted if he'd try changing.

Inside, the cabin was hot and stuffy and smelled of dust. I dug through the cupboard under the east window until I found the metal first-aid box. It contained a burn salve as well as bandages, but I couldn't remember anyone in the family ever using it. Hoping for the best, I brought everything back to the cook shack.

"We could cook the wieners now," Baily said. "The coals are just right."

"Can you eat, after this?" I asked. I squeezed salve on his blisters and carefully covered them with bandages.

"Spider will be hungry," Baily said. "All the excitement probably improved his appetite."

"I ought to poison him," I said. I looked past Baily and saw Spider ambling along the shore and humming to himself, as if nothing had happened. "A box of rocks has a longer attention span than he has. I ought to shove him in the water."

"He can't swim, remember?" Baily said, laughing a little while he inspected his bandages. "And he'd start that screeching again."

"I know," I said. "His voice is like a fingernail on a chalkboard."

We exchanged a glance, and Baily held my gaze a heartbeat too long. I looked away, confused.

I'm leaving tomorrow, I thought. There's no time for this. I barely know him, and I won't get to know him any better. I bent and snatched up the sticks he'd brought from the woods.

"Spider, you get back here and make yourself useful!" I shouted at the boy.

Spider, caught picking wildflowers and sticking them in his hat, shot up and looked around in panic as if he'd forgotten where he was.

"Hopeless," I muttered. "He's hopeless."

"Hopeless," Baily echoed. But he was looking at me.

We ate the hot dogs I cooked. Spider, anxious to help and make amends, managed to set two wieners on fire before Baily ordered him out of the cook shack until the meal was ready.

"I'm beginning to like lukewarm pop," Baily said when we finished eating.

"Justine always brought us ice from town," I said.

"Who's Justine?" Spider asked lazily as he stirred potato chip crumbs around on his plate with one finger. He had that sullen look again, as if he wanted to make an argument out of anything I said.

"Justine was our caretaker," I said. "She took care of

the place in winter, and then, just before we came in August, she checked over the food and made sure everything was all right."

"She was your maid, then," Spider said. He gnawed on a fingernail.

"She was *not*," I said. "We did our own work. She had a job at the hotel until it burned down, and she wouldn't have had any more time for us. She was very busy."

"Then what happened?" Spider said.

"Hmm?" I gathered plates and put them in the stone sink, then pumped water over them to rinse them. The big pot of water on the stove top had been warmed by the dying coals. I soaped each plate, set it on edge in the sink, and poured warm water over all of them at once.

"I said then what happened, after the hotel burned down," Spider said. His voice had a sharp edge.

I faced him, puzzled. "Oh, you mean what happened to Justine? She needed full-time work, so she moved to Seattle. Why?"

Spider's smile didn't extend as far as his eyes. "Just asking," he said. "It seems like black ladies can always find something to do."

I stared. "Are you trying to make one of those race things out of this?" I asked. "Are you trying to make it sound as if we took advantage of Justine because she was black?"

Spider shrugged. "Did you?"

"Justine is black?" Baily asked, scowling. "You never said the caretaker was black, Jocelyn."

"She did, too!" Spider said. "She did tell us the

caretaker was black. I remember!"

I shook my head. "Well, I *don't* remember, and I don't know why I would have mentioned it. What difference does it make? Don't try accusing me of being prejudiced. One of my best friends is black."

Spider cackled and rolled his eyes. "Gee, Miz Jocelyn, I never heard anything like that before. I'm gonna run off to the slave quarters and write that down so I can remember to tell my kids what a fine white lady you were."

I sucked in my breath and then let it out. "I bet you get beat up at least once a day," I said. "Ever since you got here, I've been trying to keep from knocking you down."

"You are one mean gal," Spider said. "I better look out."

"You've got that right," I said.

"Shut up," Baily said with menace. *"I'm too goddam hot to put up with this shit!"*

His voice echoed across the lake. The ducks rose from the island, quacking, and flapped east.

Spider presented his back to us and I returned to my dishes.

"Jeez," Baily said, wearily. "Enough's enough. I'm going down to the lake and soak my hand. It's starting to hurt again."

"The lake might not be clean enough," I said. "I don't think you should do that."

"What's going to make it dirty?" Baily demanded. "The hotel is gone. Your family hasn't been here for two years. As long as nobody's around, nothing gets dirty!"

"That's not true," I protested, but Baily wasn't listening. He walked toward the lake rapidly. I watched while he picked up the swimsuit he had been using and disappeared inside the cabin.

I turned on Spider. "Listen, you little creep," I said. "I don't know why you're trying to start trouble, but you'd better quit. Maybe you think I'll put up with anything because I'm afraid you'll tell the police I'm here. But if you do that, I'll tell them whatever I have to, true or not, and then you'll find out exactly what real trouble is. Am I making myself clear?"

"Yeah," Spider said. His voice was calm and controlled. He didn't blink or fidget.

He had changed. No, that wasn't it. In that instant, I had seen him for what he was. Dangerous.

"Do you know Justine?" I asked. "Is that why you were arguing about her?"

"No," he said. "You think black people all know each other? Like there's a limited supply of us?"

"Then why are you making this big deal about her working for us?" I demanded.

He blinked, shrugged, and gnawed on a thumbnail. "No big deal," he said. He rearranged his hat and pulled it lower on his forehead. The wildflowers had wilted and hung over his eyes. "You still planning on leaving here tomorrow?"

If that was an attempt to catch me off guard, he failed. I went on wiping the plates with a soft old towel. "I won't answer any more of your questions," I told him. "There's too much talking around here."

Spider got to his feet. "That's okay," he said. "I'm

going down to the lake to keep an eye on your boyfriend. Isn't it dangerous to swim right after you eat?"

I saw Baily swimming toward the island. What a dumb thing to do. He wasn't that good in the water.

"I'll go out in the boat," I said. "You finish cleaning up here. It won't hurt you to help out more than you do."

I ran toward the boat, tempted to call out to Baily and tell him I was coming. But it would be better not to distract him. I kicked off my shoes and shoved the boat into the water.

While I rowed toward Baily, I looked back to shore. Sunlight reflected off the cabin windows, turning them into sheets of gold. The cabin looked as if it was on fire inside. Spider watched me from the cook shack. He was too far away for me to see the expression on his face, but his hands were on his hips.

I glanced back over my shoulder. Baily knew I was coming and was treading water.

"Are you okay?" I called.

"I'm fine," he answered.

"If you're tired, you can hang on to the boat," I told him.

"I'm fine!" he repeated. But he sounded tired.

I eased the boat up next to him. "Grab on," I said.

He held up his blistered hand. "I can't."

"Use one hand," I said. "Do you have to be so pig-headed?"

He shook water out of his hair like a dog, and headed toward the island again. Resigned, I dipped the oars into the water.

"If you get in trouble, I'll rescue you," I said, knowing I was infuriating him. "I've had lifeguard training."

I passed him and dug the oars in deep. In a few moments, the boat nudged the shore, and I jumped out, dragging the rope behind me. On the far side of the island, an inhospitable goose honked a warning.

Baily reached shallow water and stood up. Water drops glittered on his dark skin. Did he know how good-looking he was? Those eyes, I thought, grinning to myself. His eyes ought to be against the law.

"I knew you'd make it," I told him. "How's your hand?"

"Fine," he said. He showed me his fingers. He had pulled off the bandages, and the blisters looked better. But still, he'd had a serious burn.

"That dim-witted Spider," I muttered.

"He's not so stupid," Baily said. He sat down and folded his arms over his knees. "I wish I knew what he's up to. But you'll be leaving tomorrow, so whatever it is, it won't bother you after that."

I sat next to him, but not too close. "I'll leave for town at one. Gran-auntie said she'd have everything arranged by two, even my plane flight."

"Why is it taking her so long?" Baily said.

I explained about my dad. "And she's not sure if she can find someone at the school over the weekend who can arrange for me to move into the dorm. I might have to stay with friends of hers. It takes time to work out."

"You said this place is yours," Baily said. "Did your grandmother leave it to you?"

I nodded. "Gran-auntie's in charge of carrying out everything in the will. Gerald wanted to know what I'd inherited, but Gran-auntie wouldn't tell him. She hates him. He told her he'd get a lawyer and make her tell him everything, but she told Dad, and Dad called Gerald and told him to mind his own business."

"It sounds as if nobody likes Gerald," Baily said. "How come you had to stay with him?"

"I guess Dad thought his two daughters ought to be able to live together until he gets transferred back here. But it's taking longer than he expected. And sometimes I'm afraid he doesn't really want to live in the States. I always lived with my grandparents because Dad was gone so much." I sighed and rested my head on my knees. "I think I'm running out of relatives. Nice ones, anyway."

"You'll be on your own in a few years," Baily said. "You're fifteen now?"

"I'll be sixteen next New Year's Day," I said.

Baily grinned. "I'm one month older than you."

"I wonder where we'll both be on our birthdays."

He didn't respond. He looked across the lake, concentrating on something. I thought he wasn't going to speak again, until he said, "Spider still thinks you're my girl."

"What did he say this time?"

"Who cares?" Baily said. "I told him not to open his mouth again."

"Didn't you tell him he was wrong?" I asked.

"Sure." Baily's face was unreadable. "But he didn't believe it."

I remained silent, even though my first impulse had been to complain resentfully about Spider's refusal to accept the truth. Maybe something was happening to me. Maybe I wasn't sorry Baily was here. If things had been different, Baily and I...

No, no, I thought. I'll never see him again after tomorrow.

"Do you see Spider anywhere?" Baily asked suddenly.

The sun was setting in a broad, blinding glare. Nothing moved.

"Maybe he's in the cabin," I said.

"No. I'd have seen him go in." Baily got to his feet and shielded his eyes against the last of the flat, bright light.

"Then maybe he's in the storage shed. His stuff is in there."

"Maybe," Baily said. "Let's go back and see. I get nervous when I don't know where he is." He held out his good hand to me and I took it.

"You're not going to swim back, are you?" I asked.

He treated me to one of his rare, devastating smiles. "I thought I'd ride along with you. I can tell you like being boss."

He didn't speak again until we were close to shore. Then he said, "I still don't see Spider."

"There's something about him that's really getting to you," I said. "What is it?"

He waited almost too long to answer, and then he said, "Are you so sure he's a boy?"

"What?" I asked. "Are you kidding?"

"No. I wish I were. I think Spider's a girl, and something's going on that we don't know anything about."

"Why do you say that?" I said. "I can't believe you're serious."

"Spider shaves his legs," Baily said. He laughed abruptly, then sobered again. "Guys don't shave their legs."

I stopped rowing. "Maybe you're right. When his shirt was wet, I thought I saw some sort of vest showing through it. Maybe…"

"I wondered, too. Maybe he's taped himself flat. I mean she. Maybe she's taped her chest flat."

I laughed suddenly, nervously. "This is too crazy. I don't believe we're talking about it. We must be wrong. What would be the point of it?"

Baily shrugged. "We could ask."

"He'll lie," I said. "If he's been trying to fool us, why should he tell the truth now?"

"You mean *she*," Baily said. "She."

I shook my head. "I can't believe it. We're wrong. We have to be."

But I was afraid we were right, and I wasn't certain what this meant. Now that I took a moment to think everything through, I could remember a dozen times when I thought Spider was more than just weird. He—she—was much too nervous, even for a runaway.

What difference would it make if we knew Spider was a girl? What was the point in the disguise?

If it was a disguise. We still didn't know for certain. And I wasn't sure I wanted to pursue this new problem. My time was almost up. If Spider was mixed up with something complicated, I couldn't afford to be involved.

"I can't let anything get in my way," I blurted.

Baily looked straight at me. "Nothing will," he said. "You'll be okay."

But I was getting scared. Running away had been too easy, even though I'd made careful plans. Nothing else had gone off as I'd planned it in the two years I'd spent in Gerald's house.

I could practically hear him talking about me, ranting at Hope, blaming everybody but himself.

And he'd be wondering if I'd told someone about him—and planning how he'd go about denying everything.

This was all too easy.

EIGHT

Spider was gone again, but we knew he—or she, if Baily was right—planned to return sooner or later because he'd left behind his sleeping bag and backpack. I watched the edge of the woods where the old road began, wishing the little troublemaker would reappear with a good excuse—or even one that was ridiculous—so I could be spared worrying.

But time is running out, I told myself. Time and the chance of being caught before I can get away. If Spider had wanted to make trouble for me, wouldn't he have done it by then? I told myself that worrying now, this late, was a waste of energy.

Spider was impossible to understand. I could not think of him as a girl and gave up trying. Whatever reason there was for the disguise probably had nothing to do with me or Baily.

I'm sick of the whole thing! I thought. I've had two years of worry and anger and frustration. It's got to end!

The dark descended gently, seeping into the great,

ancient hollow. The first stars flickered, weak and uncertain, in both sky and lake. The water lay still.

Without speaking, I brought out the last of the tall white candles. Baily leaned against the door frame and watched me light them. When I was done, he said, "Are we going out in the boat again?"

"Of course," I said. "We always go out in the boat for a while in the evening."

That was the last time I'll light the candles, I thought as I pulled my jacket around my shoulders. The peaceful Augusts at the cabin have come to an end. Even if I return someday—but I won't—it couldn't be the same. I don't even understand what is changing here, but something is. The last pages are being turned. And I can't bear it. It's like the heron's nest all over again. Something perfect will be gone, out of reach forever. Out of sight. And the worst part of all is that someday, when Gran-auntie's gone, I'll be the only one left in all the world who remembers what it was like in this place. Then I'll truly be alone.

I had left the boat tied to the railing, and it tipped when I jumped in. For a moment I expected to fall into the water. I couldn't seem to get my balance, and, panicked, I slipped to my knees on one of the cushions.

"Are you all right?" Baily asked.

"Yes," I said. "Of course. I think Spider's clumsiness must be catching." I crawled to my seat, embarrassed. "All I need is to drown on my last night here."

He jumped in lightly and the boat barely rocked. "You're too good a swimmer. Who taught you?"

"First Grandpa, then swimming teachers. It's the only sport I'm good at."

He sat down in the stern and shoved the boat away from the railing with his good hand. "We don't know much about each other," he said.

"No." I didn't add that there was no point. After Monday we'd never see each other again.

He didn't say anything more either, and I suspected that he had been thinking the same thing. It was better that we stay the way we were.

Tomorrow at this time I'll be in San Francisco, I thought. The nightmare of my life in Gerald's house will be over. I'll forget all about it. I'll even forget this weekend.

I rowed smoothly out to the middle of the lake and rested on the oars. In a few moments, the last of the ripples caused by the boat disappeared, and we floated on the mirror of the night sky. Once again the moon seemed to hang below the surface of the water, a mysterious lantern glowing in an unknown world.

The candles on the railing burned steadily. The flames above the candelabra glimmered on the ornate silver. The cabin seemed to be adrift, abandoned in the midst of a great hush at the end of the world.

"Tell me again about your grandfather singing to the people in the boats," Baily said.

So he, too, has found something in the past that is worth reliving, I thought. I made myself as comfortable as I could and told him once more about the candlelit boats coming single-file through the chain of small lakes, to gather, rocking gently, between the cabin and the island.

Grandpa always wore white shirts, I said, and he would step out of the cabin with his guitar, put one foot up on a bench, and sing.

When I finished, Baily said nothing, but I saw him looking east, toward the other lakes, as if he expected to see the boats coming. It was too dark to read his expression, but I was certain he wasn't smiling.

"Why are you always so serious?" I asked.

He took his time answering. "I never thought I was too serious," he said finally. "How can you be *too* serious in a world like this one? The only people who are happy are the ones who are crazy."

"That's not so," I said. "I was happy before I came to Seattle, and I certainly wasn't crazy then. Now, I'm not so sure. Sometimes I feel even crazier than Gerald."

"You were a kid before," he said. "Your grandparents were alive, and they took good care of you."

"You make it sound as if no one took good care of you when you were a kid," I said. I moved the oars a little so the boat turned halfway around. The ripples on the water shattered the moon's reflection into a million silver coins.

Baily didn't respond. Instead, he asked, "What will you do when you get back to San Francisco? School won't start for at least three weeks, will it?"

"I haven't made any plans about that," I said. "I can't until I know where I'll be staying."

"And you won't ever come back to Seattle," he said.

"No," I said. "Probably not. At least I hope not."

He stirred restlessly. "Nothing ever stays the same."

"No. But I wish it could. Some things, anyway. I wish this place could have stayed the way it was forever. But the woods across the road and the old hotel are gone. So are most of the people who made everything so special."

A light, cool wind ruffled the water. The flames on the candles stretched tall and trembled. It was time to go in, but I sat still, watching.

The last night, I thought. If only I could capture this peaceful moment somehow, and remember it exactly whenever I need to feel this way again.

"Let's wait out here until the candles burn down," Baily said.

He felt it, too. The end of something important.

"If something should happen," he said, "if your great-aunt can't work out anything and you have to go back to Gerald's house, then what will you do?"

I looked up at the moon. "But I won't go back. No matter what, I won't go back to Gerald's house. No one can make me. I'll call Gran-auntie tomorrow, just like we agreed, and if something's gone wrong, if Dad wouldn't make her my guardian..."

I stopped and shook my head. "That couldn't happen. When Gran-auntie tells him that I won't stay in the same house with Gerald one more day, Dad will let me go back to San Francisco. I'm sure of it. If I'd asked her to talk to him before, I'd already be there. When I tried telling Dad about Gerald, I suppose he thought I was only out of sorts about something. And Gerald has this way of making everything I say sound like a lie. But now Dad will know I'm really serious, since I already called Gran-auntie and she already agreed. I mean, it's practically all arranged. Isn't it? Don't you think I'm right?"

"I think it would have been better if you'd told everybody everything," Baily said. "Your dad would get you out of there fast if he knew the truth. If he knew Gerald hits on you. That's what's going on, isn't it?"

Childishly, I clapped my hands over my eyes, as if I could make everything go away. *Baily knew.* How had I given myself away? Or had he read my mind? I often thought he could. And now what? Did he despise me? Did he think I'd asked for it? Gerald always said I did.

Okay, I'd handle this, too. "I'm not sure Dad would believe me," I said. My voice shook a little, but I forced myself to go on. "Maybe he wouldn't. He might think Hope was right, that I was trying to make trouble. But I couldn't tell Dad. Or Gran-auntie. It's . . . it's embarrassing. And they're so old. How are you supposed to say something like that to people their age who might not even know what you were talking about unless you showed it to them on a videotape?"

"Just. . .just tell them right out," Baily said. He sighed. "Look, tell them Gerald made passes at you. They'll know. You won't have to describe it."

"I was afraid Dad would want me to tell exactly what happened."

"You won't know until you talk to him."

"You make it sound easy," I said bitterly. "How would you like it if you had to tell your dad—no, your mother— that somebody was always opening your bedroom door, trying to catch you in your underwear? Or that he had this way of accidentally brushing his hand over your chest. Or your legs. How would you like to *look* at your mother if you had to say something like that?"

The boat rocked gently. Baily sighed again. "Okay, I see what you mean. But you would be talking on the phone to your dad. Wouldn't that make it easier?"

"No. I even thought of writing it in a letter, but then I wondered how he'd feel when he got it. He's so far away. And what if his secretary opens all his mail? Or what if the letter got lost and somebody else saw it? And what if it came back because I didn't put the right postage on it or the stamps fell off, and Gerald opened it? He opens my mail, all of it. He says it's his Christian duty."

Baily laughed abruptly and fell silent.

"And I couldn't tell Gran-auntie. I'm sure she's never heard of anything that disgusting. And she's been so sick. What if hearing something like that made her feel even worse?"

"Couldn't you tell somebody at school? The nurse? The guidance counselor?"

"You know them. Would you?"

"No, I guess not," Baily said. "No. Not as long as I could handle everything. I mean, you were handling it, weren't you?"

"Yes. I could make him stop. But he got really mad. And he didn't give up."

"What did *he* have to get mad about? Did you sock him?"

"A couple of times," I said. "Mostly I yelled. I yelled loud enough for everybody on the block to hear me. A long time ago, Grandma told me to start screaming and yelling if anybody ever tried doing something to me that was wrong. Gerald hated that."

"And your sister didn't do anything?"

"Most of the time she wasn't home. She's got all these church meetings at night and sometimes on weekends, too. I got worn out, fighting with Gerald."

"I can see why," Baily said. "He's a pig."

He was worse than that, I thought. He got crazier every day.

Look what you make me do, Jocelyn.

That day, the day the heron died, had been terrible from the beginning. Hope had gone shopping, taking the boys with her for once, and Gerald didn't waste a minute. He caught me as I came out of the laundry room, pulling me against him, hurting my ribs.

"How come you always smell so good?" he said. His spit hit my face and I pushed him away.

"Leave me alone!" I yelled. "Let go or I'll hit you. I'll scream so the neighbors hear."

He wouldn't let go, so I grabbed the roll of fat on his neck and twisted it until he shrieked and jumped back.

"I'll tell my dad if you don't quit pawing me," I shouted. "I'll go to your next prayer meeting and tell everybody there."

His face swelled and shone with sweat. I thought he might die right there in the hall outside the kitchen. I hoped he would.

"You let the boys at school touch you," he wheezed. "Don't deny it. That's what all you girls do. If I ever catch you messing around with one of them, I'll…"

"You'll what?" I yelled. "What can you do? You're old! You're my sister's husband, and the things you try to do to me are disgusting! If I tell people, they'll throw you out of the church."

He was gasping for breath. "I'm no blood kin to you," he said. "You girls, you flaunt yourselves and then you scream when a man…when a man…"

I pushed past him and hurried outside, slamming the back door behind me. Part of me had hoped the neighbors would be standing outside in their yards, staring at the house. But part of me dreaded anyone finding out what Gerald wanted from me. He'd make it sound as if it was all my fault. But no one was around, either to help or to despise me.

Then Gerald came out. He didn't look at me or speak one word. I saw him put the chain saw in the back of his truck, and I hoped that wherever he was going it would be far enough away so that if he had an accident, no one would hear him call for help.

He cut down the heron's tree that day. He knew I'd know why.

"I don't want to talk about Gerald anymore," I told Baily abruptly. "Even thinking about him spoils every-thing."

"Some of the candles have burned out," Baily said. "Look."

I shoved the oars into the water. "Let's go back before the last of them go out. I don't want to be here in the dark."

"Let's build a fire," Baily said. "Let's build a big fire in the cook shack and light up the whole place."

"Sometimes we had a midnight supper. Are you hungry?"

"Starved," he said. "What is there to eat?"

I laughed as I bent over the oars. "We'll go through all the canned stuff and pick out anything you want," I said. "We'll have a feast."

"Well, we can pretend it's a feast," he said, laughing too. "After I leave here, I'll never eat canned food again."

The boat bumped against a piling, and I stood up to grab the porch railing. Baily climbed over and reached down to take my arm.

"Be careful of your blisters," I said.

"They're okay," he said.

When I had both feet on the porch, Baily gripped my arm a little harder, then moved his hand suddenly to my face, brushing it against my cheek. The last candle guttered and blinked out.

"My dreams can't come true," he said.

"What?" I asked.

He didn't answer. He touched one finger to my lips, and stepped back. "I'll build the fire," he said.

Then he was gone, hurrying away from me into the safety of the dark.

I stood on the porch watching until the first sparks flew upward, before I went inside to light a lantern and choose our meal. I carefully avoided thinking anything at all, except that this would be the last midnight supper.

I heated water so we could have coffee with our

dessert. It was nearly midnight, but Baily kept the fire fed with short, dry logs. Even though it was August, I could feel autumn in the night air. Summer was nearly over here. And the pile of firewood was almost gone.

"I'm almost afraid to ask, but how old are these cookies?" Baily asked.

I chose another cookie from the tin. "If I tell you, promise you won't get mad."

Baily laughed. "They aren't bad. But they have to be at least two years old, so I'm wondering if I ought to go straight to the emergency room when we've finished."

"The hospital's closed," I said. "Remember? Spider told us that."

"I wonder where he is?"

"I wonder if he's a he," I said. "But no matter what, I bet he's stuffing himself with fast food somewhere. You're still worried about him, aren't you?"

"Right now I'm only worried about getting food poisoning from these cookies."

"They can't be dangerous," I said. "There're probably full of preservatives. Doesn't that sound delicious? Anyway, the tin was still sealed. We brought two back from the gift shop in Grandma's favorite hotel, and we ate all the cookies in the other one the last time we were here."

"Is your grandma's favorite hotel the same one your great-aunt wanted you to stay in?" Baily asked.

"Yes," I said. "We always had the same rooms. Mine was on the corner, and I could see Puget Sound from the windows on one side and down Fifth Avenue from the other, and at night I could watch people lining up at the theater. Grandma would come in to watch with me when we weren't going ourselves, and she'd always say, 'Isn't this beautiful? Nothing's more exciting than a city at night.' "

"You stayed at that old hotel with all the marble in the lobby and the palm trees in the restaurant," Baily said. He laughed. "Jeez, you're spoiled."

I laughed, too. "I know it. Well, I was, anyway. Everything always worked out. Do you know what I mean? There never was any trouble that somebody couldn't fix."

"Except your grandparents died," Baily said. "Nobody could fix it when they died."

I sipped my coffee. "No. But now I'm going back, and everything will be all right again, even if I have to live at school. Other girls do it. Then when the time comes, they live at college. Nobody *has* to live with relatives."

"No more trips to Seattle," Baily said. "No more nights standing at the hotel window and watching people going to the theater. No more nights drifting around the lake." He sounded almost inexpressibly unhappy. He was the lonely dragon again.

Tears caught in my throat. There'll never be a night like this again, either, I thought.

"You're right," I said. "No more nights at the lake. What about you? Do you have plans for yourself after you get out of high school?"

"I'll go to college," he said. "Somewhere as far away from Seattle as I can get."

"Why?" Suddenly I laughed. "Because of Gerald?"

He laughed and shook his head, drank coffee, and laughed again. "Nope."

"Don't you like your parents?"

He shrugged. "Of course I do. But we're different. My brother is more like them, so he wanted to live at home when he was going to college. I just want…I don't know. Something different." He concentrated on the fire.

"What?"

He shrugged again. "Not what my dad calls 'the academic life,'" he said, and he laughed abruptly. "Reading books for the sake of reading books. That's okay for him—and my brother. But, well, my uncle has a ranch in Montana. Cattle and horses. I like it there. I'd like to be a vet in a place like that. Everywhere you look there's sky and mountains." He sighed and pushed his hair away from his face with the back of his hand. "You can be alone there and *know* you're alone. You can hear the silence."

He doesn't fit in anywhere else, I thought. He's too quiet. Nobody knows what he's thinking and so he makes people nervous, even his parents. It's hard for me to keep secrets, but it's easy for him.

My dreams can't come true. Why did he say that? Did it mean anything? Or was it just something boys like him said, mysterious boys who were too different for their own good—or anybody else's?

I could ask him to write to me. He probably writes good letters. Maybe even romantic letters. No one ever wrote me a letter like that. I've never had a real boyfriend. I can count on one hand the number of times I've been kissed, and not once did the right boy kiss me. Baily could be the right boy.

No, it's too late for anything like that. I should have

paid attention to him weeks—months!—ago. But then my heart would be breaking over him tonight. He's like somebody in a story. Not nasty, like Gerald. Why didn't I notice before?

"What are you thinking about?" Baily asked.

I blinked and looked away from him. "It's late," I said. "Don't put more wood on the fire."

"Maybe Spider will need the light to find his way back," Baily said.

"Do you think something happened to him?"

"No. I'm only worried about what he's up to. He's so weird. Sometimes I think he's our age, and sometimes I wonder if he's made it out of grade school yet."

"He's smarter than we thought he was," I said. "Especially if he really is a girl and got away with fooling us for as long as he did."

"He's too smart, maybe," Baily said.

"For all we know, maybe he came back while we've been sitting here gorging on these delicious cookies."

"You're kidding," Baily said. "Can you imagine him not barging in and grabbing all the food in sight? If he'd eat a Ding Dong, he'd be crazy about these cookies."

"You're right." But I still felt uneasy. Where was Spider? He'd been gone a long time.

Were we better off with him or without him?

Was he a girl? Or did it even matter?

$\mathcal{N}$INE

$\mathcal{I}$ slept in my clothes again. Even if Baily hadn't been around, I still wouldn't have worn pajamas to bed. Runaways sleep in their clothes, I thought, because they never know when they'll need to start running. And somehow, night seemed the time when the worst things of all might happen to me.

But even at home—if Gerald's house could be called that—I'd often slept in my clothes. Gerald had done that to me. His habit of bounding into my bedroom without warning had taught me to be anxious about my privacy, so anxious that finally I had installed the bolt on my door.

Now that my escape from him was nearly accomplished, I ought to have been more at ease, but instead I could almost feel him thinking about me, wondering where I was, sorting through the different possibilities.

And planning how to punish me. Gerald would be planning things. He liked brooding and plotting. He seemed to enjoy working himself up into a vindictive state of mind where finally he didn't seem to remember what had originally angered him, but was instead striking sparks off everything and everyone.

"He's sick," I had told Hope once. "Can't you see that? He scares me because he's got such an awful temper."

"He has to be strong and forceful or other people will take advantage of him," Hope had said. "That's how the world is, so you'd better grow up."

I'd been gone since Friday morning. Hope probably wouldn't have left for her ten-day retreat, and she'd be weeping and whining on the telephone to her friends. But Gerald would be sitting hunched over, tugging on his fat lower lip. Planning. Thinking about me. Wondering if I'd told what he had tried to do.

I heard Baily making himself comfortable for the night outside the cabin door, and then I heard nothing more. I turned over restlessly, punched my pillow, sighed. If I'd been alone, I would have climbed out of bed, wrapped up in a blanket, and gone outside to watch the stars.

This was the last night. By the following afternoon I'd know my future.

The cabin seemed to grow colder. Usually the nights didn't cool down that much until the end of August, when it was nearly time to pack up and go home. By then the lake would be strewn with slender yellow willow leaves. And in the last week, we always saw geese flying south in the early mornings.

I sighed and sat up. I needed another blanket if I wanted to be comfortable enough to sleep. The moment I switched on my flashlight, I heard Baily stir outside the door. He must have had trouble sleeping too.

"You okay?" he called out.

"I'm fine," I answered. "I need another blanket, that's all."

I could have asked him if he was cold, but I decided against it. His sleeping bag would be warm enough. I pulled a thick wool blanket out of the window seat next to my own and spread it over my bed. But still sleep eluded me. In my mind, arguments I'd had with Gerald and Hope repeated themselves over and over, and I couldn't stop them. I was almost free of them! Why couldn't I stop torturing myself?

Suddenly I heard Baily scrambling about on the porch. Before I could sit up, I heard Spider shriek, "Stop! Stop it! You're hurting me!"

I almost fell to the floor in my hurry to get out of bed. "What's wrong?" I shouted.

I fumbled with the door, finally got it open, and rushed outside barefoot. Baily had Spider pinned to the side of the cabin. "What's going on?" I demanded.

"I caught him looking through the window," Baily said. Spider tried once more to get loose, but Baily jammed his shoulders against the cabin wall. "Stand still or I'll break something," he growled.

"I was only looking to see if you two were still here," Spider cried. "I've been gone so long I thought maybe you'd taken off. How was I supposed to know Baily was out here acting like a watch dog?"

"I guess it turned out to be a good idea, didn't it?" Baily asked.

"Oh, let him go, Baily," I said disgustedly. "Spider, you make me sick. What's the matter with you? Where have you been? Why did you bother coming back?"

Baily released Spider, and Spider shook himself as if ridding himself of a burden. Baily positioned himself between Spider and me as if I needed guarding.

"Which question you want answered first?" Spider asked me indignantly.

"Take your pick," I said.

Spider rubbed his arms. "I've been in town, and one thing led to another. But I had to come back because my stuff is still here."

"So pick it up and get out," Baily said. "You didn't need to come snooping around the cabin."

"You wanted to see if Baily was inside with me," I accused. "You're some sort of nasty little peeping tom."

Baily growled something and moved toward Spider, who immediately began screeching again as he backed away.

I clapped my hands over my ears. "Don't sock him, Baily," I said. "It's not worth the effort. Spider, get away from the cabin. I'm not even going to ask what you were doing in town all this time. I don't care where you go or what you do, but I'm tired of you."

"Jocelyn," Baily said. His voice carried a warning.

"I don't care if he's told somebody I'm here," I said. But I did care. My problems were almost over. If Gerald or Hope came now, they could still complicate everything.

"Did you tell anybody about Jocelyn?" Baily asked Spider.

"About the two of you shacking up, you mean?"

Baily lunged at him. "There's nothing to tell!" he yelled as he grabbed Spider again. "Are you nuts? Where do you get these ideas?" He shoved Spider against the wall so hard that Spider whimpered.

"Okay, okay," Spider whined. "I made a mistake.

"I've been sleeping out here at night!" Baily yelled. "Can you get that through your skull? Out here!"

Now I was as angry as Baily. "How dare you even think something like that about us!" I cried furiously. "What do you think I am?"

I had caught Spider's total attention. He quit rubbing his arms and stared at me. "Oh," he said, sounding as if he'd been punched in the stomach. "Is that the truth? Listen, don't lie to me now, girl. Don't you tell lies to me now."

"You *did* tell somebody about me!" I shouted. "Who did you tell? The police? Do they know I'm here?"

"I didn't go anywhere near the police," Spider babbled. "Swear to God, I didn't."

"Then where have you been?" Baily said. He moved toward Spider again, and the boy cringed against the cabin, throwing his arms up over his face.

"I been around," Spider whined. "You know, here and there, doing stuff. I hung out at the grocery store for a while, and then I went to the diner, and then I found this all-night place where they've got twenty flavors of home-made ice cream…

"You've been *eating* all this time?" I asked. "Eating?"

"Well, practically the whole time. But I brought stuff

back. Look, see the sacks? I got stuff for breakfast again—
you don't have to eat any more of that canned junk. And I
got some of that gunk to put in the little stove I found in
the shed so we don't have to build a big fire in the cook
shack. We can have hot food any time we want. Let me
show you. You're gonna love it."

"Get away from me," I said. I shoved him hard, and
then sat down abruptly at the small table on the porch and
burst into tears. "I can't stand any more of this. Both of
you, get away from me. Leave me alone."

I could not stop the sobs that tore out of me, and I
cradled my head in my arms. It was all too much. I had
been here too long. Gran-auntie had been right—a hotel
would have been better. I could have picked up the phone
anytime and called Gran-auntie to find out what was going
on. Maybe I even could have found Dad and explained to
him as much as I dared. Maybe I could have told him
everything, and he would have believed me and not
blamed me if Hope suffered as a result. But at that
moment, I felt as if everything was coming apart and I had
failed, failed, failed.

"Come on," I heard Baily say to Spider. "Let's leave
her alone. Show me the stove and I'll fix her something hot
to drink."

"I…" Spider began, and he sounded desperate.

"Do as I say!" Baily cried. "You've screwed up enough.
If you do one more thing to her, I'll make you sorry you
ever came within a million miles of this place. Now move!"

The porch trembled as they walked away. The night
was colder than any I had ever known here. When I raised

my head, I saw that the lake shone with glacial moonlight. It looked unfamiliar, even hostile, the sort of lake one might expect to see on a distant, cruel planet. The moon looked heavy, as if it might crash to earth.

Spider came back, jittering, rubbing his arms, batting the end of his long nose. "Look, I'm sorry," he said. "Can I do something for you? Anything? Baily's fixing you instant coffee, and I brought chocolate cookies back from town. You want some? You want anything?"

He smelled like onions, and I felt like slapping him, the babbling, twitching, whining jerk. What was it about him that made me angry enough to have such violent thoughts? Was it just because he did things I didn't expect?

But at the same time, he was pathetic. At that moment, I could believe Spider was a girl playing out some sort of strange role and making herself a nervous wreck.

When I didn't answer, Spider said, "We could light some more candles out here and have a party. You know? A good-bye party? That would be great. Do you have any more candles?"

I stared at him for a long moment, and then shook my head. Suddenly I was worn out. "No, no more candles. I used them all."

"Well, that's okay, sure it is," Spider babbled. "I got some candles. I always bring candles when I come here, you bet. You never can tell what'll happen to a flashlight. Maybe the batteries will leak all over your stuff, you know? Burn holes in your clothes, maybe even your skin. You wait here and I'll go out to the shed and get the candles and come right back. Don't you worry about anything. We're going to have a nice party, and you'll feel a lot better."

Lighting candles again is a stupid idea, I thought. But why not? What difference did it make? I found my denim jacket and shoes, and pulled them on. I could see a small, dancing flame in the cook shack, where Baily was heating water. Spider was out of sight in the dark, but in moments he returned with both hands full of tall white candles. While I watched, he set them around the railing nearest the table and lit them.

"I got paper plates in town," he said. "And paper napkins. And two kinds of cookies and some candy bars and even a bunch of those green grapes that make your face pucker up. I bought doughnuts for breakfast, but if you want them now, that's okay. Doughnuts sound good to me, but anything you want is okay, Jocelyn."

"You sure have a lot of money to spend," I said rudely.

He didn't respond, but only looked at me haplessly for a moment before savaging his hangnail again. I had hurt his feelings.

"Never mind," I said. "Just never mind." Baily was coming, carrying three mugs on an old, dented tray.

"Party time," Spider said, dancing nervously. "This is going to be fun. There's nothing like a party..."

"Oh, shut up," Baily said. "You okay, Jocelyn?"

"Fine," I said. "Let's sit down. And Spider—don't talk. Don't say anything, don't explain anything. Just shut up for once, because I'm ready to kill you if you don't."

His eyes glinted, and I thought he was close to tears, but I hardened myself against feeling pity for the poor little creep. He made me too nervous. Even if he hadn't gone to town to tell anyone about me, he still put me in jeopardy. What if someone was looking for him and had caught him and demanded to know where he'd been staying? I couldn't imagine him keeping any sort of secret—except his own.

The cookies were as good as homemade, and I ate several quickly. I was developing an appetite as bad as Spider's. If I wasn't careful, I'd start talking as much as he did, too.

The candles burned straight in the still air, and after a few minutes, the lake no longer looked as sinister. I could see the Milky Way overhead, something I never saw in town.

I was too hard on Spider, I decided.

"This is nice," I said. "The cookies are wonderful, and hot coffee tastes so good on a cold night. Thanks, Spider."

He cleared his throat and smiled. "Anytime, Jocelyn."

At that moment, in the soft light of the candles, he looked like a girl. There was something about the slant of his jaw, his eyebrows, even his upwardly-curling lashes that looked more feminine than masculine. I was tempted to accuse him, thought better of it, and sighed instead. Whatever Spider's secret was, I was probably better off not knowing.

"Maybe you'll be home tomorrow at this time," Baily said to me. "All this will be behind you."

"Where's home, Jocelyn?" Spider asked.

I nearly snapped at him. But instead, I said, "San

Francisco. I'm going back to San Francisco." What harm could it do to tell him now?

"I've never been there," Spider said. "I've never been anywhere, hardly."

I passed the cookies around again. Baily took one and Spider took two.

"Is San Francisco nice?" Spider asked me.

"Yes," I said. "I liked living there. The worst times I've ever had were after I moved to Seattle."

"Won't you miss your friends?" Spider asked.

"I didn't make many," I said. "Gerald didn't want me to have friends."

"Who's this Gerald?" Spider asked.

Baily drew a breath, as if he wanted to speak, but I said, "It's all right. What difference does it make now?" I turned to Spider and said, "He's my half-sister's husband. I've been living with them because my mother and grandparents are dead and my dad works in Europe."

"Then who will you stay with in San Francisco?"

"My grandmother's sister lives there, but she's in a retirement home and I can't stay with her," I said. "She's finding me a place."

Spider cleared his throat again, harshly. "What does this Gerald do to make you hate him so much?" he asked. He sounded nervous, as if he was about to hear something he dreaded. Once again, I thought his expression to be more like a girl's than a boy's.

"What business is it of yours?" Baily interrupted.

Spider took a bite of his last cookie. "It's none of my business, I guess."

"He wouldn't leave me alone," I said in a loud voice. "I didn't mind doing most of the work around the house. I didn't even mind having to take care of their bratty boys. What I hated was how Gerald was always—how he was always touching and patting and bumping and nudging me. And coming into my bedroom when I wasn't dressed. And then praying over me at the dinner table, asking God to keep me from sinning. I wasn't having any trouble not sinning. It was him! Him!" My voice had raised steadily, until finally I was shouting. I stopped, embarrassed, and stared down at the table.

"Oh, God," Spider whispered brokenly. He turned his head away and looked out over the lake for a moment. "Didn't you tell your sister he hit on you? Why didn't she stop him?"

"She didn't believe me."

"So you came out here with Baily..."

"I didn't *intend* coming out here with *anybody!*" I cried. "Will you get that stupid idea out of your head? Baily's only been trying to help me. We aren't what you think we are. Have you got it straight? Have you?"

The candlelight glinted on a single tear that ran down Spider's face. "I'm sorry, Jocelyn. I'm sorry. I've got it straight now."

"What did you do in town?" Baily asked suddenly. He leaned over the table and grabbed Spider's wrist. "What did you do? Go to the police?"

"No, no!" Spider cried. "I told you that. I didn't go near them."

Baily dropped his wrist. "You better be telling the

truth. I'm taking Jocelyn into town tomorrow afternoon, and if there's any trouble, I'll come looking for you, and I'll find you. Now go on, get away from the table. Go to bed and don't even think about leaving here again until Jocelyn's gone. Understand me?"

Spider got to his feet, opened his mouth as if to say something, but ran off instead. No one said good night to him.

"Do you think he told anybody?" I asked Baily when Spider disappeared into the dark.

"If the police know about you and he told them you were here, they'd have come for you already, I bet. But he might not want to risk talking to them. Not in person. What if they started asking questions about him?"

"I worry that he'll say something about me to the people in the stores. Everybody knew my grandparents and me." I clasped my hands so tightly they ached. "If someone came to town asking questions about me in the stores, they might remember what Spider said."

"We've got tonight and then tomorrow morning," Baily said. "That's not so long. We can make it."

"Now I'm afraid to go to sleep," I said. "Someone could come and I wouldn't know until it was too late."

"We'll sit up all night, then," Baily said. "I'll make more coffee, and we'll sit here until morning."

"It's too cold. Let's build a fire in the cook shack and wait there."

"What about Spider?" Baily asked.

"Let him freeze," I said, swallowing my impulse to feel guilty. "I still think he's lying about what he did in

town. There's something about him that gives me the
creeps, something more than his maybe being a girl. I
know he's hiding something, but I can't even guess what
it is."

"Yeah," Baily said slowly. "I'll be glad when this is all
over. Someday we'll remember this weekend and it'll seem
funny."

"Not to me," I said. "I can't imagine ever laughing
about it."

Baily shrugged. "Okay. You're right. I was going to say
I'd write you a letter after you get to San Francisco and
we'd have a big laugh over everything, but I see your
point. It's been awful for you."

I grinned. "You could still write the letter. It just
might take me a while to want to talk about this. You
could tell me what's going on at school, how my friends
are, things like that."

"Sure," he said. "Sure, I can do that. And you could
write back and tell me about San Francisco."

He won't write, I thought. He's only being nice, trying to cheer me up. Why would he even want to remember me and all the trouble I've caused?

"We'd better clean the place up," I said.

Baily carried the mugs and I carried the rest of
Spider's feast. We left the candles on the railing burning,
and later, when Baily's fire turned the night almost festive,
I watched the candles flicker and dance in the sighing
wind that had come up when the moon sank out of sight
in the west.

Even though we had not invited him, Spider came,

finally, but he kept his distance. He crouched outside the cook shack, watching us and the fire, sniffling and coughing. Once I was certain he was weeping. But I had hardened myself against him again, and when Baily reached for my hand and held it in both of his, I didn't give Spider another thought.

We had less than twelve hours to go. Our circle of light was surrounded by darkness, and when it seemed to me that the darkness had grown more intense and drawn even closer, I kept my fear to myself.

$\mathcal{T}$EN

$\mathcal{B}$aily and I stayed awake all night, sitting side by side in the cook shack. When the darkness finally faded, I made instant hot chocolate for both of us on the small camp stove. We watched in silence until the eastern sky bloomed pink and violet moments before sunrise.

"Look," I said. "See all the colors? Sunrise is more beautiful here than any other place."

The flaming edge of the sun rose over the mountains. The island seemed to float like a pale bouquet in the clear air above the gilded water. Earlier a few birds had chattered in the woods. Now a great hush fell. It was as if the world had drawn a deep breath and waited, waited.

Suddenly the silence split open. Dozens of geese rose all at once from behind the island. They called raucously, urgently, while they flapped in a ragged circle. Then, while Baily and I watched, they cast themselves higher and formed a rough, wavering **V**.

"It's too soon for them to fly south," I said. I jumped to my feet. "They shouldn't leave for two more weeks."

"Winter must be coming early," Baily said. He got up, too. "It was so cold last night. Maybe they're smart to leave now."

"So are we," I said. "I wouldn't want to go through very many nights as cold as the last one. Do you want more hot chocolate? Or would you like to have breakfast now?"

"Sure, let's eat. Should we call Spider out of the storage shed?"

I shook my head. "No. We don't even know if he's there. Maybe he left again."

"I'll go see. We should keep track of him." Baily put his mug on the table, sighed, and stretched.

"Your hand!" I cried, grabbing Baily's wrist and holding it while I examined his burns. The blisters were infected. "Why didn't you say something? You've got to see a doctor."

Baily jerked free. "It's not that bad. Don't fuss over me. I'll be fine."

"No. We have to find a doctor. If there isn't one in town, then we'll go somewhere else. You can't let this go any longer."

"Jocelyn!" Baily said sharply. "I'll take care of it this afternoon, after you leave. Or I'll wait until I'm home. Now I'm going to check on Spider. Let's have something to eat. Time's running out."

I shrugged, but I wasn't convinced. Baily's hand must hurt, and I ought to insist that he go home now. I watched him lope toward the storage shed, and I was filled with regret that I had not succeeded in making him leave the

cabin on the first day. He'd lied to his parents for me, and
he'd been burned and must be in pain. Maybe someday
he'd think about what I had cost him, and he wouldn't
find me worth the trouble.

People—and creatures—who get too close to me get
hurt, I thought.

When Baily and Spider came out of the storage shed
together, they were arguing again. Baily's voice was low
and gruff, Spider's shrill and protesting. He flapped his
arms violently and stumbled over his feet, nearly falling.
Baily didn't offer help.

"Moron," I muttered, and went to work. The water
bucket by the sink was full. I set it on the stove before I
poked through the ashes, looking for enough hot coals to
simplify building a new fire.

"Here, let me do that," Baily told me as soon as he
reached the cook shack.

"No, it's a two-handed job," I said.

"I'll do it!" Spider cried. He jittered and danced from
one foot to the other, fussed with his hat, plucked at the
front of his baggy shirt. "Let me do it. I can build a fire. I'll
do it, Jocelyn!" His eyes were bloodshot and he coughed
incessantly. I could tell he'd been crying again too.

"I'm already doing it," I said. "Set the table, why don't
you?"

"Remember, I got doughnuts and grapes and stuff,"
Spider said. "We'll have to eat everything up if we're going
today. Oh, look at Baily's hand. Jocelyn, did you see his
hand? We've got to do something about it right now."

"It's okay," Baily said. "Stop jabbering about it."

"I think he should go to a doctor," I said.

"Yes, yes," Spider babbled. "We'll go into town right away and get a doctor for him. We'll find one. Somebody'll know where. We'll all go, right now, and eat breakfast in town. Don't you think so, Jocelyn? Don't you? Shouldn't we go now, before his hand gets any worse?"

"Will you please be quiet?" Baily said. "You sound like all your wires came loose at the same time. Nobody's going anywhere until Jocelyn's ready to leave this afternoon. Understand that? Nobody leaves."

"But your hand," Spider said. "We gotta do something about your hand. We got to leave."

Baily impaled him with a cold, mean look and Spider shut up, snuffling.

"Jocelyn," Baily said, "what's the bucket of water on the stove for?"

I fed thin strips of kindling into the fire, coaxing it along. "I want to wash all the dishes and pans we used before I put them away," I said.

"You're like a fussy old lady, the way you take care of this place," Spider said. "Why waste all this time?"

Without looking at him, I said, "I suppose I could treat this place the way you would—throw the garbage in the lake and leave everything dirty. But I'm doing it my way, and I don't care what you think." I could have added that the closer the time came to leave, the more frightened I got, and the only way I could control my fears was to follow Grandmother's careful, neat ways. But I couldn't afford to appear vulnerable in Spider's eyes. He—she—might still be the source of disaster.

Spider fidgeted, ripping at a hangnail. "How are you getting back to San Francisco, Jocelyn?"

"On a plane," I said. I lit the camp stove again and put a small pan of water for coffee on it. "Set the table," I told Spider again.

But he dawdled, fussing with paper napkins, folding them into fantastic shapes almost blindly. "You got a plane ticket already?" he asked me.

"Why?" I asked, testing the water in the bucket with one finger. It was still cold, of course. The fire smoked and sulked, and I added more kindling.

"Somebody's getting a ticket for you?" Spider asked. "Somebody in Seattle?"

I whirled and stared at him. "Why do you want to know? So you can sneak off and tell?"

"No, no, no!" he cried. "I'm not telling anybody anything about your plane ticket. If you've got one. Maybe you don't have one yet."

Baily stepped toward him. "Stop talking," he said with menace.

Spider concentrated on setting the table. He perched the blue paper napkins, folded into the shape of long-necked birds, beside the plates. Another time, in another place, I would have told him how clever I thought he was. I had tried dozens of times to fold napkins like that and had only succeeded in frustrating myself. Maybe Spider really was a girl—it didn't seem to me that a boy would care about anything like that.

Grandma could fold napkins into fancy shapes.

"Where did you learn how?" I had asked her once, after giving up the task myself.

"Justine taught me. You should see the roses she makes out of linen napkins for the hotel. She's really artistic."

"Am I artistic?" I had asked.

"You are everything that's wonderful," Grandma had said.

Oh, Grandma, I thought as I watched Spider fussing over the table. What would you think of all this?

By the time we finished breakfast, the sun had climbed over the mountains. The sky curved bright and empty around it. There had been swallows darting over the lake the day before and now they, like the geese, were gone. A small flock of mallards paddled busily between the island and the shore, leaving ripples behind them on the glassy water. The heron was back, though, standing in the shallows and peering into the water.

"Jocelyn," Baily said. He stood beside the post where my height had been recorded year after year. "Stand here for a minute. I'll carve a new mark for you."

For a moment I wasn't certain I wanted to leave a record of this visit to the lake. And it didn't seem right that anyone except Grandma would carve the mark on the post. But Baily had his knife out, trying to open it, fumbling with his injured hand.

"Here, let me do that," I said. I opened the pocket knife for him and stood straight against the post. He made a light cut and I stepped away.

"I've grown in two years," I said.

Baily deepened the mark, cutting out a thick slice. "Maybe I should carve the year here, too," he said. "Would you like that?"

"No," I said, with more emphasis than I had intended. I didn't want that. The post would seem like a grave marker then.

Baily shrugged. "Suit yourself, but it wouldn't take long."

"There won't be anybody to see it," I said.

I bit my lip to keep from crying and began gathering up the mugs and plates from the table. I'd clean up the cook shack and the cabin before I left, just as if I'd be coming back next year. Work would make the last hours pass faster, and I wouldn't worry so much. Now that it was almost time to call Gran-auntie, my fears surged back. What if Gran-auntie hadn't found Dad? What if she wasn't my guardian yet? What if she couldn't find a place for me to stay—or the school wouldn't take me back?

I could have handled my problems with Gerald a better way. If I had told…no, I'd been over and over that in my own mind before I made my decision to run.

Spider wandered aimlessly along the shore, scratching bug bites, fussing with his hat, coughing. Baily, one-handed, gathered scraps into the plastic trash bag we would dispose of in town.

"We should pull the boat in and put it back in the storage shed," he said.

"Not yet," I said. "I want to go out on the lake one more time before we leave." I looked over my shoulder at Baily. "You're tired. Why don't you try to sleep for a while?"

"I'm no more tired than you are," he said.

But he seemed drawn and tense, and I saw him look in Spider's direction more than once.

"I don't think he'll run off now," I said. "Anyway, it's nearly too late for him to do any damage. If he'd meant to hurt me, he'd have done it already. He or she. Whatever."

But Baily didn't answer and he didn't laugh at my weak attempt at a joke. He merely watched Spider, leaning against the post, his expression unreadable.

I soaped the dishes and coffeepot, and dipped warm water out of the bucket to pour over them. After I dried them, I stacked them on the old tray and carried them back to the cabin. The ritual comforted me.

It wouldn't be possible to wash the sheets and blankets this time before storing them in the window seats. I slid everything into plastic bags and put them away. I took the batteries out of the lanterns and flashlights, returned them to their places, and closed all the cupboards. I kept only the silver candelabra, which I wrapped in a clean towel and put in my duffel bag. It felt almost like stealing. But there was no one else to keep it safe.

I looked around the cabin carefully to make sure I had taken care of everything. Then I changed clothes, pulling on tan slacks and a thin pink cotton shirt.

These clothes will be all right for the plane, I thought. I won't be too wrinkled by then. Anyway, what does it matter how I look?

I folded my denim jacket and put it on top of everything else in the bag. All done, I thought.

Suddenly my eyes flooded with tears. How can I leave this place behind when I know I'll never come back? I thought. Why does everything have to change? Isn't there something I can do to fix things? No. There never was a way. I have to face it and accept it.

I rubbed my eyes on my sleeve and left the cabin. One more walk around, and one more trip across the lake in the boat, then good-bye, even if it breaks my heart.

Baily had gathered up his belongings and stacked them near the porch steps. He stood midway between the cook shack and the cabin, watching Spider, who was dragging his things out of the cook shack.

"What's wrong?" I asked Baily.

"I'm not sure," Baily said. "He still wants to leave right now. He keeps harping about it."

"Because of your hand?"

"That's what he says," Baily said. "But there's something else going on. He's really anxious to get out of here. I wouldn't be surprised if he took off without us."

"You think he might have turned me in last night," I said. "Right?"

Baily shook his head. "The police would have come already," he said. "They wouldn't have left you out here if they'd known about you. At least, I don't think so."

"Then what's bothering you?" I asked.

"Nothing, I guess," he said. He wouldn't look at me, but I knew with certainty that he wanted to.

Spider trudged in our direction, carrying his backpack and sleeping bag. "Do you want to go now, Jocelyn?" he called out hoarsely. "Maybe we ought to leave before it gets too hot."

I shook my head. "No."

Spider dropped his belongings and gawked at me. "Why not?"

I wouldn't tell him about calling Gran-auntie. It was none of his business, and I still feared giving him too much information. "I want to go out in the boat once more before I leave."

"Then let's do it now," Spider said. "Yes, that's a good idea. Let's go right now."

"Later," I said.

Spider yanked on his hat. "Okay. Okay, then. Maybe I'll go for a walk."

"Leave your stuff here," Baily said quietly.

"I was going to!" Spider cried. "You think I'm going to take off, don't you? Well, you're wrong. I need to be by myself and think for a while."

"With what?" Baily growled. "You make so much racket you must have killed off your brain years ago."

Spider opened his mouth, then shut it again. He turned his back on us and lurched toward the shore. We watched while he made his way east, toward the far end of the lake.

"Jerk," Baily said under his breath.

We walked in the opposite direction without speaking. I looked at my watch every few minutes, until Baily told me I couldn't make the hands move faster by staring at them, no matter how hard I tried.

"I could go into town early," I said. "I could call and see if everything's set up. Maybe it is. Maybe it was all taken care of yesterday and I could have left then."

"Stick to the plan," Baily said. "It would be a mistake to change anything now." He looked over his shoulder, and I turned too. Spider was nearly out of sight.

"I wish he weren't such a nervous wreck," I said. "It makes me nervous watching him."

"Who can tell what's going on with him? Why the disguise? I'm sure he's a girl, but what's the point? And that smart-ass attitude of his when he first showed up, when he behaved as if this place was rightfully his."

"I know," I said. "But if he really did come here before, he didn't do any harm. And he couldn't get inside the cabin or the shed. Not that it would have made any difference. There isn't anything worth stealing."

"I'm not so sure he intended to be alone here," Baily said slowly.

I stared at him. "You think he was expecting somebody to be here? Somebody he knew?"

"He brought two cinnamon rolls, remember?"

I laughed. "Yes, but he's a perfect pig. He eats everything but the napkins and plates."

Baily laughed too. "You're right." He looked back once more, then at me. "I won't stop worrying until I see you get back on the bus."

"I won't stop worrying until I'm on the plane and it takes off," I confessed.

"I could go to the airport with you," Baily said suddenly. "Just to make sure everything's okay and nobody else is hanging around."

I held my breath and worked hard not to grin. Finally I said, "I guess that would be all right."

But then I laughed suddenly. "What if Spider decides to go along with us?"

"Don't even think about it," Baily said. "He's so crazy

he would attract too much attention."

"Can you imagine what would happen if I tried to go through security with him acting the way he does?" I said. "Nobody would mistake him for a hijacker, but I think they've got rules about just how weird a person can be before they let them near a plane."

"I won't let him go with us," Baily said. "I promise you that."

We reached the western end of the lake and turned back. In the distance, all the ducks suddenly rose from the water in noisy flight.

"Something must have frightened them," Baily said.

"No," I said. "See? They're leaving." Overhead, the ducks wheeled once over the lake and then turned south, into the sun. I blinked back tears and said, "The sky's so bright it hurts my eyes."

But Baily didn't notice my distress. "There's Spider," he said.

I saw him then, too, heading toward the cabin. Or toward us, perhaps. I couldn't tell from such a distance. We watched while he hopped on one foot, then sat down abruptly on the grass, pulled off his shoe and shook it vigorously. Next, he appeared to be fussing with his shoelaces. His cough sounded worse, almost like a dog's loud bark.

"It's time to go back," I said. "I want to make sure the fire is out before we leave."

"I put it out already," Baily said. "I poured water on the ashes, too."

I smiled up at him. "You're a good camper," I said.

He stopped walking and looked down at me soberly. "Jocelyn," he said.

I blinked.

He smoothed my bangs away from my forehead. "What's this place called? Doesn't it have a name?"

"Summerspell," I whispered. "Grandma called it Summerspell."

"That's what it is," he said. "Three days of magic and you're going away, and I'll never see you again."

"We don't know that."

"Oh yes, we do," he said. "We know it."

I wished he would kiss me so I could kiss him back, but he didn't. I knew that the right moment was lost to me.

Spider looked up from his knotted shoelaces, hoarsely yelled something I couldn't make out, and waved to us. We walked on, side by side, not touching. Carefully not touching.

ELEVEN

Spider, waiting by the porch and blinking nervously, thrust a bouquet of wildflowers at me and smiled.

"Here," he croaked. "I'm sorry I'm such a knothead. I don't blame you for being mad at me."

I took the flowers, and noticed that the skin around several of his fingernails was raw and bleeding. He seemed near tears again. Trapped between exasperation and laughter, I thanked him, but I had no idea what I was expected to do with the bouquet. Wildflowers always wilted within moments of being picked, so I certainly couldn't take them with me. And what would be the point of sticking them in water and leaving them behind in the cabin?

Baily solved the problem. "Why don't we put them in a can of water in the cook shack?" His sober expression was unreadable. If he thought Spider was acting like an idiot again, he kept it to himself this time.

"That's good," Spider said, with relief so obvious that I felt sorry for him. "Yeah, that's a great idea. Let's do that now, and then we can leave. Okay, Jocelyn? It's time to go, right?"

"I'm not leaving until one o'clock," I said.

Spider's head jerked around and he looked back at the overgrown road through the woods, almost as if he had heard something.

"What is it?" I asked. My heart thumped. I couldn't be caught now! I was almost safe.

"The crows in the woods make a lot of noise," Spider said.

I hadn't heard them, and I didn't believe Spider had, either.

"You're up to something," I said. I took a step toward him. "What is it? You'd better tell me right now."

"I'm not up to anything!" he cried. "Why are you always blaming me for things?" He backed away from me, stumbled, and bumped heavily into the porch railing. The railing cracked ominously and then, before he could regain his balance, it sagged away from him.

"Look out!" I cried.

Spider shrieked and fell backward into the water. The lake was only a few feet deep there, and if he had simply stood up, he would have been safe. But he panicked instead, splashing wildly, choking and screaming.

Before I could react, Baily leaned out over the water, grabbed the back of Spider's T-shirt, and pulled him close to the porch. For a moment, I thought Baily might fall in, too, so I knelt quickly and dragged Spider out of the water.

"You weren't in any danger!" I yelled at him. "You made everything worse by acting like such a..." I stopped and stared.

Spider's T-shirt had been pulled up around his shoulders. He tried yanking it back in place, but I saw what he was trying to hide. His chest was wrapped with layers of elastic bandage. Now we knew for sure! Spider was a girl.

"Don't you try to hide!" I shouted. I reached to pull the T-shirt back up, but Spider held it down and struggled to get away from me. Baily grabbed him and twisted him around to face me.

"You *are* a girl!" I shouted. "Baily, look at that bandage! See what he's done? He's strapped himself—*herself*—flat! We were right!"

We had suspected the truth, but now, faced with it, all my anxieties turned to fury. If it was the last thing I did here, I'd find out what Spider was up to.

Spider jerked free from both of us and backed up against the cabin wall. "So what if I'm a girl? What of it? What business is it of yours what I do?"

"Who are you?" I shouted. "You'd better tell me right now. Who are you, and what are you doing out here?"

Spider clasped her arms across her chest. "I'm doing the same thing you're doing," she said. "Only I'm not taking chances, that's all."

"What's that supposed to mean?" I demanded.

"Guys hit on girls when they're traveling alone," Spider said. "You know that!"

I remembered the problem I had with the guys in the bus station, so I nodded.

"Sometimes it scares the hell out of me," Spider said. "Sometimes I'm broke and I have to hitchhike, and then it's even worse. You think Gerald is the only pig out there? Where've you been, girl? My own sister told me how to dress to be safer. Hardly anybody bothers me when they think I'm a boy."

"Except," Baily drawled, "you forgot boys don't shave their legs."

Spider stared at him. "How long have you known? Why didn't you say something instead of letting me go on?"

"At first I couldn't believe it," Baily said. "And I didn't want to worry Jocelyn until I had you figured out."

"And now I suppose you think you do," Spider said, sullen. She was shivering so hard her teeth chattered.

"Why don't you make it easy and tell us, then?" Baily asked.

"There's nothing to tell," Spider said. She coughed and wiped her eyes with the back of one hand. "We all ended up at the same place at the same time, and I didn't see any reason to tell you anything you didn't need to know."

"Start with your name," I said. "I need to know that, since you've been staying at my place."

Spider's gaze dropped. "My name's Marsha."

"And you've been here before," Baily said.

"A few times," Marsha began.

"Baily, your hand!" I interrupted. I grabbed his wrist. The blisters were bleeding and his hand was badly swollen.

"Don't," he said, and he pulled his hand back. "It's okay."

"I'm sorry, I'm sorry," Marsha cried. "You hurt yourself pulling me out of the water. Let's leave now and find a doctor. You've got to see a doctor. Come on, come on!"

Baily turned on her. "Why? What's the hurry? What difference does it make if we leave now or in a couple of hours? What's the problem?"

Marsha backed up, blinking. "No problem. No problem at all, except your hand. It must hurt. I only wanted to help. That's all I ever wanted to do."

"Go put on dry clothes, Spider or Marsha or whoever you are," Baily said. "You're a mess."

Marsha glared at him, but she didn't argue. Baily and I watched her flounder toward the storage shed and then we exchanged a disgusted look.

"I suppose she's right," I said. "That it's safer if people think she's a boy when she's traveling alone this far away from Seattle. There were two guys pestering me in the bus station on the way out here, until a woman made them quit. But I'll bet nobody started in on you."

"Spider would be safe traveling bare naked with her hair on fire," Baily said bitterly. "She's at least half crazy. Anybody talking to her for more than five seconds would only want to run screaming in the opposite direction. I think she's a natural-born sneak. She likes fooling people. It's some sort of power trip for her. She laughs behind people's backs, I bet."

I looked thoughtfully after Marsha. "I think you're right—about it being a power trip for her," I said. "But still, I wish I knew why she's really here. I know she said she's running away, and that she's come here before, but still…I don't know." I looked at my watch. "Well, it doesn't matter. It's nearly noon. I'm leaving in an hour, and none of this will matter. I hope."

"Jocelyn," Baily said.

I looked up at him. "What?"

"Everything's going to work out fine."

He's got such beautiful eyes, I thought. My breath caught in my throat.

"Come inside so I can bandage your hand," I said gruffly. "Let me do that much for you."

He followed me inside and sat on a window seat while I pulled out Grandma's first-aid box, and he held up his hand cooperatively while I spread ointment on it and wrapped it in gauze.

"I'll worry about you when I'm gone," I said. "I'll wonder about your hand."

"I'll be okay," he said.

"You said you'd write," I reminded him. "Did you mean it?"

I glanced up and found him staring straight into my face. He laughed a little and looked away. "I meant it. At least, I'll write if you promise to write back."

I nodded. "I'll want to hear about your hand."

He looked back at me again. "Yes," he said.

Marsha stumbled over the doorsill and tottered in. She wore loose gray shorts and a baggy dark blue T-shirt. Her hair was slicked back again, and shoved under her wet cap. Her damp shoes squeaked on the wood floor.

"I can't believe you left that wet bandage on under your shirt," I said. "You aren't fooling anybody anymore."

"Hey," Marsha said, shrugging. "It's my style. What can I tell you? We all got our style."

Unwillingly, I burst out laughing, and after a

moment, Baily laughed, too. Marsha lifted her chin indignantly for a moment, and then she, too, surrendered and
laughed.

"Oh, girl, I got style," she said. "You better believe I
got it." She put one hand on her hip and strutted back and
forth in front of us, scrawny shoulders swaying, long nose
in the air.

"I believe you," I said. "Trust me, I can see you've got
style."

"You know that story about the ugly duckling?"
Marsha asked, posing in front of us, her legs all sharp
angles and knobs, elbows poking out into space. "You
know the part where she turns into a swan? Well, that's
what I'm going to do—turn into a swan, any minute now.
Don't you blink or you'll miss it."

Baily shook his head, but I laughed. "I think you'd better find yourself a fairy godmother, because right now, wearing those colors, you look more like a heron, with those
long legs and the way you flap your arms around," I said.

Instantly I was sorry I had made the comparison,
because Marsha's smile faded a little.

"I don't know a heron from a hummingbird, but I'm
going to believe you're giving me a compliment," she said.
"I think both of you look nice, too."

I winced. I liked homely, awkward Marsha better
than shrieking, obnoxious Spider, but neither of them
could ever have been my friend, and I felt guilty.

"You okay, Jocelyn?" Baily asked.

"I'm fine," I said. "Let's go out in the boat."

Baily got in first and offered his good hand to me.

Both of us helped Marsha, who fussed over the seating, the cushions, and a spot of dampness she found on the deck, which she was certain meant the boat would sink immediately and who knew what was waiting under the water to grab us. I rowed out to the middle of the lake and warned Marsha to be quiet.

The boat sat still on water that reflected perfectly the hard, bright sky. Fat white clouds hung motionless overhead. Nothing moved anywhere. Not even a bird broke the silence.

Spider—Marsha—sat in the stern, looking north, with her cap pulled low to shield her eyes from the sun. In the bow, Baily had stretched out on the deck and lay, eyes closed, with his head propped on a ragged red and white cushion. I thought he might have fallen asleep. His injured hand lay across his chest, and rose and fell with his easy breathing.

I told myself that I would have to fix all of this perfectly in my memory, to keep forever. If Gerald had not taken my camera away from me, I could have snapped pictures of everything, even ridiculous Marsha, scowling and gnawing on her fingernails. I smiled to myself. Exasperating as she was, Marsha had added something to these last minutes at Summerspell. For a few moments I had felt like a teenager again, instead of someone who had grown much too old in only two years.

"Jocelyn," Marsha said. Her rough voice was soft for a change.

"I told you not to talk," I said. She was spoiling the moment.

"This is important," Marsha said. She squirmed in her seat, crossed and recrossed her legs, picked at a bug bite.

"Okay, what is it?" I said.

Marsha pleated the fabric in her shorts with nervous fingers, coughed, and didn't say anything more.

Goosebumps ran along my arms. When Marsha looked up at me, I had a sudden, terrified impulse to tell the girl not to say anything more.

"I know who you are," Marsha said.

I heard Baily's sharp intake of breath and I realized he was not asleep. His eyes opened and his gaze found me.

"Okay, so you know who I am," I said. My voice shook a little. I don't want to hear this, I thought. Please, don't say anything more. Let me go on believing I can get away from Gerald. Because that's what this is all about. She's going to tell me I won't be able to get away, and all this has been for nothing.

"You're Jocelyn Tyler," Marsha said. "And I'm Justine Poe's daughter."

"Oh, no," I said. My mouth trembled. Justine, the caretaker. "What are you doing here?"

"My mother sent me," Marsha said. She rubbed one hand over her mouth, as if she wanted to stop herself from going on. "The old lady in San Francisco, your great-aunt, she got hold of Mama and told her you'd be staying here by yourself for a few days, and she was worried about you, so she asked Mama to come out and make sure you were all right. But my sister, Angela, she just had a baby, and Mama had to take care of her when she got out of the hospital, so she sent me in her place. She knows I've been here a few times. She told me to come and stay with you until today, and make sure you were safe."

I licked my dry lips. "Why didn't you tell me who you were as soon as you got here?"

Marsha's gaze dropped to her bitten fingernails. "I didn't tell because of Baily. I saw the two of you here together, and I figured that somebody had been lying. You were supposed to be running away from this mean man— at least, that's what Mama thought. She didn't know who or why, just that you were in trouble. But here you were, with a boy, and you didn't look like you had any problems except the kind that would make that old lady mad if she knew about it."

"We told you over and over again that you were wrong about us," I said.

"I didn't believe it," Marsha said. "It sounded like something you made up because you were ashamed of what you were doing."

My ears were ringing. I was angry, but I was also frightened—because I knew Marsha was frightened.

"What have you done?" I asked the girl.

Marsha wouldn't look at me. "I went into town to call Mama and tell her what was going on. To tell her what I thought was going on, anyway. But I couldn't reach her the first time."

"Sunday morning," I said. "You're talking about yesterday morning."

"Yeah. So I had to go back again."

"What happened?" I cried.

"I told Mama that you were here with a boy and you didn't seem like you were in trouble. What else could I have said? It looked like the truth."

I clenched my fists in my lap. "But it wasn't. Did you call her again and tell her you were wrong?"

"It was only when I got back here that I found out how things really were, and it was too late then," Marsha said.

I pressed my fingers against my lips for a moment. "What did Justine say?"

"She was mad, like I knew she'd be," Marsha said. "She really loved your grandmother and her sister. She said she wasn't going to put up with you cheating on that nice old lady by running off with some boy and then expecting her to rescue you from getting what you deserved."

"What do you mean, what I deserved!" I shouted. "Justine didn't call Gran-auntie and tell her that garbage, did she? She wouldn't do something like that!"

Marsha shook her head. "Mama didn't want to worry her, her being so old and all."

"So?" I urged. "What was she going to do, then?"

Marsha's eyes filled with tears. "She said she had to call your sister and see what she wanted done with you. Mama thought maybe your sister would let you go back to San Francisco anyway, so she wouldn't have to be responsible for you since you mixed yourself up with a boy, but Mama wanted to be sure."

"How did she know about Hope?"

"Mama always had her name and number." Marsha

coughed violently for a moment. "Your grandmother gave
her a list of people she could call in case there was ever an
emergency out here."

I gritted my teeth. "Why didn't Justine mind her own
business?"

A tear dropped straight down Marsha's cheek. "Mama
was mad at you, can't you understand that? She thought
you were trying to pull something over on that old lady."

Baily got up on one elbow. "We'd better leave. Now."

"Marsha, does your mother know I'm going to call
Gran-auntie at two o'clock? If she knows that and tells
Hope, Hope and Gerald might wait in Franklin Springs for
me. It's so small they can find me, especially since I have
to get a bus at the depot. I need to go somewhere else, find
some other way of getting to Seattle, and then maybe call
Gran-auntie from there."

"I don't know if Mama knew all that," Marsha said.
"She didn't say anything to me about it. I was supposed to
come here and stay with you until you knew what you
were going to do next. Last night she told me I could go
back to Seattle anytime I wanted, because you had all the
company you needed if you were with a boy."

I ran both hands through my hair distractedly. "I
don't know what to do. I can't think straight." I stared at
Marsha for a moment and then shook my head. "What
have you done?" I asked again.

"If you'd told me how bad that Gerald is," Marsha
began. "If you'd explained…"

"She didn't owe *you* an explanation," Baily said. "She
didn't owe you anything at all."

"I was trying to do what Mama said and protect the old lady," Marsha said. "Jocelyn, listen to me. Remember when you told us about the best time you ever had? Remember? Seeing the boats with the candles coming and your grandpa singing? Well, it was my best time, too. Mama took Angela and me out in a boat one year, and I saw all that. I saw you, too. You had everything! I knew all about your rich grandparents, your famous grandpa, your private school. We were the same age, and you had everything and I didn't have anything! I used to come out here with candles and light them and pretend I was you. I wanted to *be* you. Jocelyn, you had everything I wanted!"

I stared at her with contempt. "Oh, sure, I had everything. Except that my mother and my grandparents are dead, and my dad—my own father!—lives and works in Europe and doesn't want to hear from me about trouble, and my half-sister loves me so much she wouldn't listen when I told her that her crazy husband wouldn't leave me alone."

I pressed my fingers against my lips for a moment to stop them from shaking. When Spider opened her mouth to say something, I broke in first. "I can't have friends unless I sneak around to see them. I'm not supposed to even talk to boys because crazy Gerald is afraid I'll end up in bed with them, and he wants me for himself. He told me so! He told me that while he was cleaning his rifle, and he aimed it at the wall and clicked the trigger. 'Somebody dirties you, I'll kill him,' he said. He reads my mail and listens in on my phone calls. I practically live in my bedroom. I had to put a lock on my door to keep him out!

And then when I try to get back where I belong..."

"Why didn't you tell anybody what was happening to you?" Marsha shouted. "This is *your* fault, too. *Your* fault! You should have told somebody what your brother-in-law was doing to you."

"I told my sister! She didn't want to hear it. I tried to tell my dad—I called him in Berlin and tried, but I didn't know how to say it, or if he'd understand, or if he'd even know what I was talking about. I couldn't tell Gran-auntie, because she's too old and sick."

"There are other people to tell," Marsha said. She was weeping hard now. "How stupid can you get? What about your teachers? The school counselor? What about your doctor? What about your neighbors?"

"Are you nuts?" Baily shouted. He sat up, scowling. "Sure, she should have told somebody. But strangers? Would *you* tell strangers? How do you go about it? Think about it for a minute, since you're so darned smart. What do you say to strangers about something like that, when the people who ought to listen to you won't do it? Her sister should have stopped it."

"Then why didn't she?" Marsha said. "Angela wouldn't let anybody treat me like that. Why didn't your sister stop him, Jocelyn?"

"Because then she'd have to do something about Gerald," I said. I slumped on the seat, shook my head, rubbed my eyes with the backs of my hands. "I don't think she wants to stick up for me because if she did, she might lose him."

"Who wants him?" Baily asked disgustedly.

"Hope does, I guess," I said. "She doesn't like trouble. She never wants a fuss."

"Then maybe she won't come out here," Baily said. He sounded as if he believed it.

I almost pitied him because he was so innocent. "Oh, Hope wouldn't come out here alone," I said. "No way. She'd come with Gerald. Or maybe she'd send Gerald by himself, so she doesn't have to get mixed up with anything, and she can pretend nothing's wrong."

Baily pushed his hair back with his good hand. "Okay, so she sends Gerald. What of it? We can get back to Seattle one way or another in spite of him. Then you can call San Francisco and find out what your great-aunt wants you to do. And you can call your dad and tell him everything this time, the whole thing. You won't have to go back with Gerald, I promise."

"Jocelyn," Marsha said. Her voice cracked. "Oh, Jocelyn."

I watched while Marsha got to her feet, rocking the boat a little. "Sit down before you tip us over," I said.

"Somebody's here," Marsha said.

$\mathcal{T}$ WELVE

$\mathcal{G}$ erald had come out of the dark woods alone, and he made his clumsy way along the overgrown road, watching his feet as he walked but stumbling in the tall grass anyway, flattening wildflowers in his path.

He wore baggy camouflage pants and a bright orange vest that flapped open as he moved. He was too far away for me to see his expression. I wasn't certain he had seen us yet.

I fought back an insane urge to laugh. Even now, even at this terrible moment, Gerald managed to humiliate me. He was ridiculous! His pants sent one message—a mighty hunter was coming, one who was stealthy and clever and invisible to his prey. His vest, however, shouted that he was afraid another hunter might mistake him for a deer and shoot him. And his hat—it was the kind I had seen Vietnam veterans wear, but Gerald had never been in military service. He carried his rifle, too.

Then I understood. Justine had told Hope I was at Summerspell with a boy. Gerald had come to force me home at gunpoint and drive off his rival.

Our worst enemies ought to appear terrifying, like the devil himself, I thought. How dare Gerald show up here looking like a...a cartoon! How could my companions take me seriously, when my enemy was such a clod?

"Is that *Gerald*?" Marsha asked. "Or are we being invaded by the Delta Force?" She snickered nervously and covered her mouth with her hand. The boat rocked again, harder this time, when she shifted her feet.

I stood up. Might as well face it, I thought bitterly. "Yes, that's Gerald," I said.

"Hoo, take a look at the big hunter," Marsha said. "The deer must get a laugh when they see him coming."

Baily moved to sit upright, but I said quickly, "Lie down so he can't see you. Maybe he won't start anything if he doesn't see a boy here."

"I don't care what he starts..." Baily began.

I panicked and put one foot on Baily's shoulder, pressing down harder than I meant to do. "Please," I begged without looking at him. "You've got to let me handle this by myself. Maybe I can keep you out of it. He won't be so mad if he thinks one of my school friends is here and we're just two girls out in a boat."

"You're not going back with him!" Marsha cried. "You'll have to run away all over again if you do something as dumb as that."

"I'll never go back. Never." I clenched my fists at my sides and watched Gerald waddle toward the cabin. *Think*, I told myself. What are you going to say to him? How can you make him leave?

Baily groaned and tried to push away my foot so he

could sit up. "Jocelyn, he can't tell Spider's a girl."

My gaze flew to Marsha, who gaped at me in return, speechless for once. *Oh God, Baily's right.* That wasn't a girl standing on the seat with her arms folded across her flat chest. That was a black teenager named Spider. A black boy.

Gerald was twenty feet away from the shore when I was certain he saw us. He stopped, shielded his eyes, and stared. The boat rotated a little, facing shore, facing Gerald.

Marsha turned her head, still watching him. Her grin was fading. Now she knew, too, that everything was going wrong all at once and there was nothing we could do, no place we could hide.

Baily pushed at my foot, struggling to rise.

What can I do—what can I say to Gerald? "Now wait a minute…" I muttered, almost to myself. My mind was blank, and I heard my pulse beat in my ears. Wait. Everybody just wait while I think of a way to get us out of here. The island. If I can get us to the island…

"What have you done, Jocelyn?" Gerald screamed at me. "Who is that nigger boy? What have you done to me?"

Everything that followed happened in slow-motion, but I had lost my voice and could think of no way to protest. I raised my hands to ward off what was coming, even though it would be impossible. Gerald brought up the rifle and tucked it into his shoulder, and now he didn't seem to be such a comic figure. Now he was all of my bad dreams come true at once, and there was nothing I could do to make myself wake up.

All in the same instant I heard the shot, felt the displaced air gush past, and saw bright red satin ribbons fluttering gracefully through the air. Where had they come from? Had Marsha been holding them rolled up in her hands? The ribbons splashed across my face and over my shirt, and then I saw that they were blood.

Marsha threw up her hands and arched backward, then fell into the water, pulling her bright ribbons with her.

The boat rocked wildly, nearly capsizing. Baily tumbled flat on the deck—When had he gotten to his feet?—and he cried out something I could not understand. I could not keep my balance and collapsed on top of him.

Then I was on my knees, clinging to the sides of the boat, my fingernails digging painfully into the wood. Where was Marsha? Gone? Gone?

Gerald. There he was, staring at me, his arms limp, his rifle at his side.

Madness. This was all insane. It can't have happened. I climbed to my feet, stood on the seat facing Gerald, and raised my fists. *You are really crazy, crazier than I ever dreamed*, I thought.

Where was my voice? Why wasn't I making a sound?

Jocelyn!" Gerald screamed. "*Jocelyn! Look what you made me do!*"

"Get down, quick!" Baily cried. He reached up and grabbed my legs. "Get down or he'll kill you, too!"

He dragged me down beside him and wrapped his arms around me to hold me there, and the boat pitched and rocked, pitched and rocked, slamming us violently against the ribbed hull. Water spilled into it, so cold it shocked me. I waited to hear the next shot, waited for the boat to flip over, too terrified to draw a full breath. Baily made a small sound, almost a moan, like an animal trapped in its den.

I wanted to hear Marsha yelling for help, shouting that she couldn't swim, demanding that we do something to put an end to this. But she wouldn't. I knew Marsha could not still be alive. I had seen what Gerald had done. What he could do.

Baily held me for a long time, more time than I could comprehend, while the boat rocked itself to sleep, and silence curled around us again, and nothing moved, and no one spoke.

At last we rose and sat side-by-side, without speaking, our arms around each other, while we saw everything there was to see. We were alone in the great shallow basin the glacier had scraped out, once upon a time.

Gradually the ripples in the water died away, and the lake was a mirror again. Beside the boat, Spider lay face down in the immense sky. Above and below, a wedge of white geese fled silently south.

I don't remember how we got to town for help, but Baily told me we ran between the trees beside the road, even though Gerald had driven away and the road was deserted. We learned later that he bolted to his sanctuary, the hunting lodge in Idaho.

The only recollection I have is hurrying, hurrying in the white-hot heat, looking desperately for my grandparents. Lost. All lost, I seem to remember crying. Baily told me I never said one word, not even when we reached the sheriff's office.

But I remember the sheriff's wife. She and I sat on her lawn swing while we waited for Baily's parents to come for us.

"I remember your grandma," she said. "And your grandpa and how he sang. Oh, my, how he sang out there under the stars. Wasn't that something?"

The old maple tree over the swing dropped gold leaves on us, and the swing creaked.

Lost, all lost.

$\mathcal{T}$HIRTEEN

$\mathcal{A}$ man passing the sidewalk café lit a cigarette and discarded his match on the pavement. A fat gray pigeon rushed at it, pecked at it twice, and turned away, disappointed.

It was past three o'clock on Friday in Seattle, and Baily stood in the long line at the espresso counter. He looked over at me and shrugged helplessly. I smiled as best I could. It didn't matter if I had to wait. I was grateful to be outside in the warm, overcast autumn afternoon.

All the blue metal tables were occupied except for the one next to ours. A folded newspaper lay there, left behind by a woman in a black suit. I reached for it and unfolded it on our table.

There was Gerald's picture. My throat tightened. Gran-auntie had refused to let me see the newspapers all week, and the television sets had been removed from both our rooms.

"You don't need to concern yourself with rubbish," she had said.

So here was the rubbish. Gerald's picture, showing him looking old and tired. SUICIDE IN IDAHO, the headline read.

My picture was next to Gerald's, but it was smaller, the same size as Spider's. Someone had found our high school yearbooks. We were smiling. I touched Spider's picture and sighed. How could you have known when this picture was taken that you'd never have a senior picture in a yearbook?

Baily brought my mocha and his espresso to the table. "What are you looking at?" he asked. "Are you supposed to read papers? Put it down, Jocelyn. If your great-aunt finds out I let you look at a paper, she'll be sorry she let me take you out for a walk."

He pulled the paper out of my hands, folded it, and stuck it under his chair. "Here's your mocha," he said. "Look out. It's really hot."

"Yum," I said. But I could scarcely taste it. What did the newspaper say about me? Did it tell everything about Gerald and me? Did it blame me?

"I like your great-aunt," he said. "But she's tough. I thought she'd never let me talk to you anywhere except in the hotel lobby with the concierge peering at us like a chaperone."

"She's very old-fashioned," I said. "She keeps me safe."

"Sure," Baily said. We both knew there had been a time when she couldn't.

"So tonight you'll be sleeping in a dorm in your school," Baily said. He looked everywhere except at me.

"Yes," I said. The pigeon was back, begging at the table behind us where a man laughed and broke off pieces of a cookie to scatter on the pavement.

"I hope you know nothing that happened was your fault," Baily said suddenly, urgently.

"You keep telling me that," I said. "But it was my fault. If I had told people…"

"You told Hope."

"I should have kept on telling until somebody listened," I said. "It was all my fault. I know that now."

"It was Gerald's fault," he said. "His and only his. He made the decision to shoot, not you."

"Shh," I said, looking around.

No one was listening. The man feeding the pigeon was laughing with his friend. At another table, three women passed around a snapshot, exclaiming over what they saw.

But beyond them, a man and woman shared a newspaper, and the woman's eyes met mine. I looked away quickly.

"That's her," the woman said to the man with her. "Look. At that table over there. It's the girl in the paper."

Baily turned to scowl at her. The woman was actually smiling.

"It's really her," she said. "The one we saw on television, remember?"

"Come on," Baily said. He got to his feet and picked up our drinks. "We'll finish these while we walk. Want to go down to the waterfront? We've got plenty of time."

I hurried beside him blindly, hearing the woman's voice rising behind me. "It's really her! It is!"

"No, I want to go back to the hotel."

"Ignore her," Baily said. "Why should you care what she says? You're leaving tonight, and your great-aunt already told you that the papers and television in San Francisco aren't paying any attention to what happened. They've got their own murders…"

"Please!" I cried. "I want to go back to the hotel."

"No, come with me to the waterfront," he said. "No one will recognize you. We'll talk and walk and not think about anything bad. It'll be okay, I promise. Come with me. We won't have another chance."

I looked up at him and he smiled at me. "All right," I said.

This was the last chance we'd have to spend time together. Summer was over.

At a quarter to eight that evening, I stood at the window in my hotel, watching people line up at the theater across the street. My suitcase was packed. The plane would leave at ten.

Gran-auntie put aside her magazine, pushed herself up from the sofa, and stood beside me. "What do you see, darling? Oh, the theater people. Remember when we saw *Phantom of the Opera*?"

"I remember lots of musicals we saw there," I said.

"What grand times we had," Gran-auntie said. She sighed and shrugged. "Heavens, we're carrying on as if we'll never buy tickets to anything again. Come sit down and rest, Jocelyn. Your father won't be here for another fifteen minutes."

"I'm not tired," I said. I watched four teenagers go through the theater door, dressed up, almost dancing in anticipation of what was to come. "Dad doesn't need to ride to the airport with us."

"Well, he wants to," Gran-auntie said. "He'll feel better if he sees you off."

"I've been getting along fine without him all my life," I said. I moved to the other windows and held back the curtains so I could see the city lights and Puget Sound. I knew the view intimately now because I had spent so many days in this room studying it.

"Jocelyn," Gran-auntie said in a chiding voice. "You're stronger than Hope. Always were. She's got such a mess on her hands now, and you're nearly free of it. A few more hours, and you'll be where you belong."

The phone rang and Gran-auntie reached for the nearest extension. "Oh," I heard her say. Then, "What? What? Well, you're going to have to tell her that yourself." Gran-auntie held out the phone. "It's your father," she said, and I knew from her voice what Dad would be saying.

"Hello, Dad," I said wearily.

"Jossy, I'm so terribly sorry to let you down," Dad said. "But I'm here in the emergency room with Hope. She couldn't seem to breathe, and it wasn't safe to leave her like that, so…"

"I know," I said. "Tell her I'm sorry she's sick, okay?"

"Well, you do understand, don't you, that I can't get away to drive you to the airport? Can you two manage? Do you want me to arrange for a car and driver?"

"Dad!" I said impatiently. "Stop it! All we have to do

is go downstairs and ask the doorman to get us a taxi. I'm sure the two of us can handle it, okay?"

"I don't want you to be upset, Jocelyn," my father said. "You've had such a hard time, and I don't want to make it worse. Are you sure you'll be all right? Will you call me as soon as you reach San Francisco?"

Wordlessly, shaking my head in disgust, I handed the phone back to Gran-auntie before I returned to the windows. The city lights flickered below, and cars streamed along the streets. A light rain, almost a mist, had begun falling, and everything looked so clean, so new.

"For heaven's sake!" Gran-auntie cried into the phone. "Now what? What on earth possesses you to upset her when we're practically out the door? What? She certainly will not call you when she gets to San Francisco. Mother Sebastian is meeting us at the airport and taking Jocelyn straight to the dormitory, and her girls aren't allowed to use the phone in the middle of the night. She'll write you a note when she settles back in school. Goodbye."

She replaced the receiver and sighed. "I hope you can be more gracious to him than I just was, even if it half kills you. But if you want to throw something right now, I won't object."

I laughed and let the curtains fall back in place. "All I want is to go home," I said. "But I'd like something to eat. Suddenly I'm starving. Is there time for room service to send up a sandwich?"

It seemed to me as if I was always hungry. Like Spider, I thought. Just like Spider.

Gran-auntie looked at her watch and shook her head. "We'll have to hope for the best at the airport. It's almost time to leave."

I returned to the window that overlooked the theater. It was eight o'clock. The sidewalk was empty now, except for one boy.

Baily. He stood there, hands in his pockets, shoulders hunched against the drizzle, looking up at my window.

My eyes filled with tears. We had said good-bye that afternoon. But here he was again, and there was no time for me to run downstairs and across the street.

He took something out from under his jacket. A long white candle. He couldn't light it—not in the rain. It wasn't possible.

But he lit it anyway and shielded the flame with his hand. Could he see me watching him? Of course. I moved the curtain a little to be certain he would know I was there.

Someone knocked on the door. "Porter," a man called out.

"Here we go, Jocelyn," Gran-auntie said. "Come along, darling."

One more second, I thought. One more second, so I know I'll be able to remember this forever. I moved the curtain again, and Baily raised one hand to wave. The candle flame nearly went out. I let the curtain drop back in place.

"We've got this bag, and that one over there, and the small one on the bed," Gran-auntie told the porter. She leaned heavily on her cane. "Am I forgetting something? Jocelyn, look in the bathroom. Did we leave anything behind?"

"No, we've got it all," I told her. I pulled on a new jacket and brushed a bit of lint off my new pants.

"You've got your book to read on the plane?"

"Yes, and yours, too," I said. "Let's go."

Will he still be there? I wondered as we rode down in the elevator. When we reached the street level, the porter signaled the doorman, who in turn signaled the first taxi in line. The doorman helped Gran-auntie settle herself in the backseat while the porter loaded the luggage. I climbed in beside Gran-auntie and the taxi turned out into the street.

Baily stood at the corner, still holding the candle. Should I tell Gran-auntie? No, this was for me alone.

The candle flame was reflected in the mist and seemed to grow larger. Tears dazzled my eyes. I pressed my hand against the window when we passed Baily.

"You comfortable?" Gran-auntie asked. "Is everything all right?"

"I'm fine," I said. I cleared my throat and swallowed my tears. "Perfectly fine."

When I looked back, I couldn't see the candle any longer, but that didn't matter. Baily Lassiter, of Seattle, Washington, had my address in San Francisco, and he had promised me that he was the world's best and most faithful correspondent.

And he had just given Summerspell back to me.